w, this **was** kiss...

betwe... ...ertips found the silky skin
skirt. He fo... ...w's short sweater and little
agreed on just a... explore farther, but they'd

So he focused on her m...
longer, harder, deeper. Only kissing her
air to pepper the corners of her m...th with ...ming up for
mini-kisses, tasting her soft skin, treating
himself to her hidden scent where her neck
curved into her shoulder.

But the kiss was a lie.

He was living a lie.

She thought he was Jeffrey, and Jeffrey
thought she was the enemy. And here in L.A.,
Jordan Adamson didn't even exist. Of all the
off-limits women in the whole off-limits
world, Ashley took first prize.

There was no way for this to turn out well.

Ashley took a step back, slipping from his
arms, breaking their touch. 'That
was…cataclysmic.'

And he *so* wanted it to.

Dear Reader,

When Colleen Collins and I decide... the big
connected books, we knew we h...ska, which is
city—her area of expertise—... of *The Parent*
mine. We came up with ...alised we were onto
Trap for adults, and ...
something fun.

Throughout ...e writing I helped her with the
Alaskan details, such as whether or not you'd find
trees on the tundra and how a dog-sledge works.
At the same time she told me about the
peculiarities of television executives and where to
eat and shop in L.A. It was an experience we'd
both like to repeat someday.

I sincerely hope you enjoy meeting Jordan
Adamson, the hero in *Too Close To Call*, along
with his long-lost twin brother, Jeffrey Bradshaw,
in *Too Close for Comfort*.

Happy reading,

Barbara Dunlop

Available now:
Too Close for Comfort by Colleen Collins

TOO CLOSE
TO CALL

by
Barbara Dunlop

MILLS & BOON®

For my dear friend Colleen Collins—
city girl extraordinaire.
And for my brilliant editor, Kathryn Lye.
We're not in Kansas anymore!

All the ch...or, and have no relation whatsoever to anyone bearing the
of the ...
so...e name or names. They are not even distantly inspired by any
individual known or unknown to the author, and all the incidents are
pure invention.

First published in Great Britain 2004
by Harlequin Mills & Boon Limited,
Eton House, 18-24 Paradise Road, Richmond, Surrey TW9 1SR

© Barbara Dunlop 2003

ISBN 0 263 84003 4

21-0304

Printed and bound in Spain
by Litografia Rosés S.A., Barcelona

1

"NATIONAL WEATHER says there's a snowstorm building off the Gulf of Alaska," Jordan Adamson called to his dispatcher in the reception area of True North Airlines as he tore the printout from his fax machine.

"Is it going to shut us down?" Wally Lane swiveled on his chair, eyebrows lifting. "Cyd's heading out on the Arctic Luck run in about ten minutes."

"We've got a few hours leeway, but radio Bob and make sure he keeps an eye on it."

Flying in adverse weather conditions was part of being an Alaskan bush pilot. Though late October snowstorms could be fierce, Jordan didn't want his pilots taking unnecessary chances. Go or no-go was a combination of meteorological reports, the view outside the cockpit window and gut instinct.

Jordan reached through the window opening from his small office and handed Wally a copy of the report. "Tell Bob to hold tight in Sitka if necessary." After a second's pause, he added, "And remind him to—"

"Keep the customer satisfied," Wally echoed the rest of Jordan's words with perfect rhythm and intonation.

Jordan rolled his eyes heavenward. The staff at his small airline in Alpine, Alaska had been teasing him for months about his evangelical customer satisfaction mission.

"Bob's picking up his ex-wife," said Wally. "He might prefer the storm to holing up with her in Sitka overnight."

Jordan grinned. "Pilot's discretion." He took a step back.

"Roger," said Wally, with a snappy salute.

The front door opened, and Wally swiveled back to the counter as a man stepped into the reception area. Jordan assumed it was Cyd's four o'clock passenger.

In that European suit and shiny loafers, the man was overdressed for a plane ride to Arctic Luck. In fact, he was overdressed for anything north of the six-tieth parallel.

The man looked up, and Jordan did a double take. There was something startlingly familiar about him. Had they met before? The man's eyes widened, and he drew back. For a moment, Jordan wondered if he'd somehow offended him.

While Wally talked to the customer, Jordan turned to the stacks of papers on his desk, making a quick search for a passenger list to check the name. Part of delivering good customer service was remembering your customers' needs and treating them as though they were important to the business. It was all right there in the Alaska Tourism Association brochure guidelines.

Jordan's airline currently held first place in this year's Alaska Tourism customer satisfaction surveys. If he could hang on to the lead for the rest of the season, it would mean free advertising in all of the government brochures next summer. That kind of exposure was sure to increase his business—a necessity if he wanted to add a commuter jet to his fleet.

Which he did.

As soon as possible.

While he located the manifest for the Arctic Luck trip, he heard Cyd land the Cessna. Right on time, but she'd have to be quick with the turnaround if she wanted to beat the snow.

Jordan squinted at the passenger name, hoping it would trigger a memory.

Jeffrey Bradshaw.

The name didn't mean anything to him. He glanced back through the window, racking his brain. He *knew* he'd seen the man before.

"JEFFREY BRADSHAW is due back in L.A. on Monday." Rachel Bowen, a set designer at Argonaut Studios stopped beside the treadmill where Ashley Baines was jogging to the beat of vintage Springsteen.

"What?" Ashley pulled off the headphones, snapping them around her neck.

"Jeffrey. Here. Monday," said Rachel.

Ashley hit the button on the treadmill control and rocked to an abrupt stop, turning to stare at her friend and co-worker. She drew a deep breath, winded from her workout. "So, that's it, then." She wiped a hand across her hair, down over her tight braid. "It's him against me?"

Rachel nodded. "Sure looks that way."

Ashley felt her stomach clench. Jeffrey showing up to challenge her for the promotion to vice president wasn't exactly a surprise, but she had held out a slim hope he'd stay away and leave the field clear.

A fellow acquisitions director at Argonaut, Jeffrey was definitely her most serious competition. He was smart, experienced and connected. He was also crafty, with a ruthless edge that she wouldn't want to test.

Perspiration tickled her forehead and her temples, and her damp spandex top stuck to the skin between her shoulder blades. She picked up a white towel that she'd hung over the handle of the treadmill and scrubbed it across her forehead, flipping her braid out of the way to dry her neck.

"Got any more scuttlebutt on him?" she asked.

Rachel was a close friend, and a gifted set designer at Argonaut. She was friendly and outgoing, and had an amazing ability to keep her finger on the pulse of office politics.

"Just that he's checking out locations in Alaska," said Rachel.

"Alaska?" Ashley blinked in confusion.

"You know. Snow, ice, you have to cut through Canada to get there."

"His big, innovative idea is *Alaska?*"

The chairman of the board had let it be known that an innovative new hit series was number one on his wish list right now. Whoever came up with the right series had a huge leg up on the promotion.

Jeffrey had spent the last year on special assignment in New York. What could have given him a sudden interest in Alaska?

"He must be pitching a *Northern Exposure* thing," said Rachel.

"A comedy?" Ashley tossed the towel into a nearby bin. Comedies were always risky, but when they hit, they hit big.

"Or an outdoor adventure," said Rachel.

"Adventure's on the decline. It's medical, cop or comedy this year."

An Alaskan cop? An Alaskan hospital? Neither of those rang true to Ashley. It had to be a comedy.

Shoot. The last thing she needed was for Jeffrey to deliver something more original than her edgy, California-based detective series.

"Think I should add a comedic element?" she asked Rachel, raising her thumb and capturing the nail between her teeth. Maybe straight drama wasn't the way to go.

"Comedy *is* big right now," said Rachel.

Of course it was. Comedies were getting all the attention this year, all the awards, all the ratings. How could she have been so foolish?

Ashley headed for the change rooms. "I should have thought of this earlier."

"It's pretty late in the game to switch," said Rachel.

"I know. It'll mean redoing the storyboard and the video clips."

"And rewriting all the scripts."

Ashley paused with her hand on the change-room door. "It'll mean redoing the *entire* presentation. From scratch." A near impossibility, since this was Saturday, and the pitch meeting with the chairman of the board was scheduled for Monday.

Rachel tucked her dark hair behind her ears. "I suppose you could take a chance to submit it as is."

Ashley's hardboiled detective drama suddenly seemed pale and flat, and somehow safe, even if it did have beaches, plenty of buff bods and guaranteed action sequences in every episode.

If Jeffrey was going for broke with a comedy/drama, set in Alaska of all places, she was going to have to make her California location feel fresher and more interesting.

"Think he's going for broke?" asked Rachel, skipping to keep up with Ashley as she headed down the tiled hallway, past the racket courts.

"Alaska's a pretty bold move for a setting," said Ashley. The more she thought about it, the more she realized Jeffrey was taking a risk, pulling out all the stops.

And, why wouldn't he? It was the promotion of the decade.

She'd made a mistake when she let his absence lull her into a false sense of security. He might not have been in L.A. all year long, but he was still a force to be reckoned with.

"Any way to put off the Board meeting?" Ashley asked. She definitely needed more time.

Rachel stopped in the middle of the hall and gave her an incredulous look.

"You know his secretary, right?" asked Ashley.

Rachel knew everybody.

"Not that well," said Rachel.

"She got any weaknesses?"

"Chocolate and Chippendale Dancers," said Rachel.

Ashley smiled. "What about *Fire Dance* tickets. I hear the male lead is burning up the headlines."

"You've got tickets to *Fire Dance?*"

"Front row, center, balcony one." Ashley's grin widened. "Clive Johnston traded me for the Lakers last week."

"Throw in dinner at La Salle, and I think I can get you a deal."

"Done," said Ashley. "Get her to switch the meeting to Friday." She stopped at the door to the change room. "You going to be around tonight?"

"You want to grab dinner and sketch out some ideas?"

Ashley nodded. "That would be terrific."

"Meet you on the deck at the Breakwater Café."

"Give me half an hour to shower and change." Ashley pushed open the door with the heel of her palm. Her workout was officially over. She now had more important things to worry about than her glutes.

JORDAN WASN'T GOING to worry about Cyd, even if she was overdue by half an hour. The storm had grown faster and more violent than anyone had predicted. The radios weren't working, but if she'd gone down, they'd have an emergency beacon signal coming in. They didn't.

She'd probably landed short of Arctic Luck.

"Everyone but Cyd's accounted for," said Wally, hanging up the office telephone and tossing his clipboard onto the counter. "Bob's holed up in Sitka, and the rest never got off the ground."

Just then an operator's voice came over the radio phone.

Jordan was closer, so he grabbed the mike.

It was Cyd. And, thank goodness, she was fine.

But before Jordan could get more than a few particulars, an angry male voice took over. "I'm the passenger who paid to be flown to Arctic Luck," Jeffrey Bradshaw thundered.

Terrific. Maybe Cyd wasn't so fine.

"But I was flown to Kati—Kati—"

Jordan didn't wait for Jeffrey to spit out the word Katimuk. He keyed the mike. "Sorry about that," he interrupted, putting on a relaxed, professional voice. "Can't fight the weather. But we'll get you to Arctic Luck as soon as possible."

"I need to get there immediately." The command crackled through the static of the radio waves.

Wally raised his eyebrows.

"Afraid we can't do that," said Jordan. Weather delays were a necessary hazard of flying in the North, particularly in the fall. Jeffrey needed to buck up and wait it out.

"Nothing's impossible," said Jeffrey. "I'll contact my office. Have them call another airline."

Jordan keyed the mike again. "You can call. But, nobody's going to fly in this."

"Why?" Jeffrey demanded.

Why? Didn't they have windows up in Katimuk? There was a good foot of new snow on the ground in Alpine, and more was gusting from the sky.

"Weathered in is weathered in," said Jordan, shooting Wally a look of amazement. What part of blizzard didn't Jeffrey understand?

Wally grinned. He'd made a big deal yesterday about how this Jeffrey guy looked exactly like Jordan. And Jordan had to admit there was a bit of a resemblance. But he was beginning to hope that was *all* they had in common.

Jordan released the mike button. "Please tell me I'm his double in looks only."

Wally just grinned wider.

The radio stayed silent.

Jordan keyed the mike again. "Nobody will risk an aircraft," he elaborated, trying not to let the frustration come through in his voice. "And I'm sure you don't want to risk your life. Stick with Cyd. She knows what she's doing. She'll get you out as soon as possible."

"Let me get this straight," said Jeffrey. "Your pilot could have landed me in Arctic Luck, but she flew me to Katimuk instead?"

Wally rolled his eyes and started to chuckle at the absurdity of the questions.

"She landed where she felt the plane and passengers would be safe," said Jordan. *Be thankful you're alive,* he almost added. Be it Katimuk or Timbuktu, safe on the ground was safe on the ground.

"Bull," Jeffrey barked.

"Charming," said Wally.

"And nothing like *me*," said Jordan.

"THERE WAS NOTHING even remotely funny about that, was there?" Ashley let her head fall back in defeat on the couch in her small Westwood apartment.

Rachel clicked a button on the remote control, turning off the last video clip for the detective series, and the television screen went blank.

"Not particularly," she admitted.

They were going to have to reshoot every clip.

"What if Detective Moonie is older, more worldly-wise, jaded..." Ashley searched her brain for possibilities. Their original idea was definitely not going to fly as comedic.

"If he's older, we'll lose the buff bod," said Rachel. "Pecs sell. You know that." She stood up and stretched her arms above her head, moving immediately into a graceful toe touch.

"So do tight butts," Ashley pointed out. "Could we have an older, worldly-wise detective with a great butt?"

Rachel straightened, pulled down her cropped T-shirt and laughed. "I can see it all now, Detective Moonie, health club maniac, near retirement and just in from the mean streets of New York, decides to take a part-time gig as a lifeguard, faces danger, thrills and jokes while chasing bikini-clad women along Malibu Beach."

"Okay, the butt would be tough to do on an old guy. What if we make him younger? But a geeky, unattractive man who's fawned over by gorgeous women. Then we're sure to nail the eighteen to thirty-five-year-old male demographic."

"The basic premise behind all of your finer adult films." Rachel crossed to the small kitchen. "Got any wine in here?"

"In the fridge door," said Ashley. "Maybe we make him gay."

"Oh, yeah, now that'll nail a broad demographic."

"I think women like gay men."

"As friends, sure. But not as a buff butt fantasy on their television screens." Rachel popped the cork on the wine bottle.

"Our demographic is men, anyway," said Ashley. "Hey. What if Detective Moonie is an aging, hard-boiled, uptight eastern kind of guy, and his new protégé is a gay, laid-back, California beach boy."

Rachel stopped, midpour. Her eyes narrowed. "That could be funny."

Ashley quirked an eyebrow. "Couldn't it, though? Fish out of water? The women in the episodes would all be attracted to the gay guy, but end up lusting after the older guy with experience."

"Think we could get Sean Connery for the older man?" asked Rachel.

"You and I are definitely on the same wavelength." Ashley curled her legs under her on the couch, her synapses starting to hum.

"YJ17546, True North Airlines answering," Wally said into the mike of the radio phone.

Jordan glanced through the office window as Wally hung a suit jacket on the coat hook in the reception area. The coat sure didn't look like Wally's style.

One of Jordan's other pilots was also out in reception, busy explaining the afternoon flight delay to six Japanese tourists. Jordan had arranged a free night's stay for them in a local hotel, and the interpreter was passing along the news.

Meanwhile, four cameras clicked away, the occasional flash reflecting off the posters on the walls.

"I don't think you understand just how serious this situation has become," came an all too familiar voice over the radio.

Jordan caught Wally's gaze through the open window, then he shook his head and pretended to bang it three times against the office wall.

"Say again?" said Wally into the mike.

"I need, *need* to be in L.A. by the end of the day. Do you understand that?" Jeffrey's voice rose. "There's almost two feet of snow up here, you have all my credit cards and *I* have to get to L.A."

"I'm afraid the snow has grounded all of our flights again today," said Wally. "What credit cards?"

"In my coat. The pilot put me in some kind of giant parka but then left *my* coat behind. What kind of an outfit is this?"

"The parka's a necessity in the Cessna. And, I can assure you, your credit cards are perfectly safe," said Wally evenly, taking down the suit jacket and putting it in his lap.

Oh, boy. Jordan made a mental note to lock Jeffrey's coat and credit cards up in his office. He also figured he'd better write a memo regarding passenger's personal effects. Not that anyone had left their clothing behind before. Well, except for the bra in the Cessna that one time.

"And, I understand your frustration," Wally continued smoothly. "I truly wish I had an easy solution."

Jordan was going to make Wally employee of the month.

"And, I truly wish you understood the problem!" Jeffrey snapped back.

Wally held the mike toward Jordan, an invitation to take over clearly written on his face.

The tourists watched the exchange with interest, cameras poised in case something interesting happened.

Jordan signaled that Wally should keep talking. He was doing a terrific job.

Wally shrugged philosophically, then mouthed "watch this" to Jordan.

"So, why don't you explain it to me?" Wally said to Jeffrey. He held up the brochure from the Department of Tourism, pointing to bullet point number five: *Let the customer vent when necessary. Ensure you show empathy before giving him any negative message.*

Jordan gave Wally a thumbs-up.

"I have an important meeting in L.A. at eleven o'clock Monday morning," Jeffrey articulated in a staccato rhythm. "If I'm not at that meeting, I will lose my promotion, and most certainly lose the Alaska television series."

"There's going to be a television series in Alaska?" asked Wally, his voice betraying a sudden interest.

"Not if I stay stuck in Katimuk, there's not."

"What kind of a television series?"

The camera clicking stopped, and the Japanese tourists all bowed to the pilot before filing back out to the bus. A couple took final shots of Wally talking on the radio.

"It would have been called *Sixty Below,* a comedy about the lives and loves of the people in Arctic Luck," said Jeffrey.

"Would. Note the word *would,*" he continued. "I never did get to Arctic Luck, strike one. I can't take pictures of anything in the blizzard, strike two. And I can't get to the pitch meeting tomorrow, strike three."

"Can't you pitch it by phone?" asked Wally as the door swung shut behind the interpreter. The pilot headed for the hangar.

"Pitch what?" asked Jeffrey. "I've never even seen the town. And, no, it's not something you do by phone. I need pictures, drawings, storyboards."

"Of Arctic Luck."

"No. Of San Diego. Of course of Arctic Luck."

Wally glanced at the wall of the office.

Jordan followed his gaze to the collage on the bulletin board. Sure enough, there were pictures of Arctic Luck, along with every other community in interior Alaska.

"If...uh...somebody else went to the meeting, with

pictures and diagrams, could you tell them what to say?"

Wally was offering to go to L.A.? Was he crazy?

"Won't work," said Jeffrey.

"Why not?"

"They won't take the pitch from anybody but me."

Jordan strolled into the reception area and leaned against the counter, crossing his arms over his chest, trying to figure out what Wally was thinking. Sure, he could take a four-wheel drive into Anchorage. The jumbo jets were still taking off near the coast. But, what the heck did Wally think he could do in L.A.?

"What if it was you?" asked Wally.

Jordan waved his hands and shook his head frantically. Making promises you couldn't keep was definitely against the Department of Tourism's wallet-card advice.

"You're sending a plane?" came Jeffrey's hopeful voice.

"No. I'm sending Jordan."

"Jordan?"

Jordan?

"My boss. The guy who looks just like you."

"Jordan's flying up here?"

Jordan's not flying anywhere.

"Nope. We send Jordan to L.A."

"What?" Jordan's sharp exclamation matched Jeffrey's.

"Holy cow," said Wally. "Even your voices sound the same."

"I'm not going to L.A.," said Jordan, moving toward the radio.

"That's ridiculous," said Jeffrey.

"He looks just like you," said Wally into the microphone. He pointed to the graph on the wall showing the customer satisfaction ratings.

The static crackled on the radio. "It's not—"

"He does," came Cyd's voice in the background.

Jordan's eyes narrowed.

"Put your money where your mouth is," Wally said to Jordan. "If you hurry, you'll be back in time for your birthday."

Jordan started to protest, but he quickly realized he didn't need to say a thing. Jeffrey would put a stop to this. Jordan could just stand here and pretend to go along for the sake of customer satisfaction. He'd be putting his money where his mouth was, without actually having to pay up. Perfect.

"Sure," said Jordan easily, enjoying the role of customer service white knight. "Anything for customer satisfaction."

"We give him a haircut," said Wally into the mike, with a thumbs-up to Jordan. "You tell him exactly what to say. He goes to the meeting, then flies back home."

"Never in a million years," said Jeffrey.

"You got a better idea?" asked Wally.

"Fly up here and get me," said Jeffrey.

"No can do. Tell me, what's the worst that would happen if Jordan tried and failed?"

"The series is dumped, and my career is ruined."

"What will happen if you don't make the meeting?"

"The series gets dumped, and my career is ruined."

"What are the odds of success?"

"Ten percent."

"That's ten percent better than we've got going for us now." Wally pointed to another bullet point on the department's brochure: *Take the customer's problem on as your own.*

Now Wally decided to become Mr. Customer Service Guru. Jordan waited for Jeffrey's vehement dismissal of the whole idea. Jordan in L.A. trying to pretend he was some hot damn television executive? As if.

"We have pictures of Arctic Luck," said Wally into the silent radio.

"Good ones?" asked Jeffrey.

"Great ones," said Wally.

There was a long silence. Jordan blinked in confusion. Where was the supercilious, unreasonable man from yesterday? He should be coming back with an angry retort about fixing the weather, telling Wally what a ridiculous, unworkable—

"First thing he needs to know is the org chart," said Jeffrey.

Jordan stumbled a step back, his eyes widening.

"There's a copy of last year's annual report in the right-hand, top drawer of the desk in my condo. Keys to the condo are in my coat pocket."

2

THE FIRST PERSON Jordan met in L.A. was Jeffrey's friend and former co-worker, Rob Emery. Nice guy. A whole lot nicer than Jeffrey seemed, in fact.

Jeffrey had explained the impersonation to Rob, and Rob had offered to help in any way he could.

They'd stayed up all night reviewing the basic makeup of Argonaut Studios and the delivery of a presentation for the television series Jeffrey had planned.

Jordan didn't get any sleep, but by morning he was armed with sketches, descriptions of scenes, outlines of the series characters and pictures of Arctic Luck for the location—all in living color. Rob, now a documentary filmmaker, definitely seemed to know what he was doing, and Jordan felt confident he could describe Jeffrey's television series proposal to the Board members.

In fact, he thought it would be a very funny show. Stereotypical Alaska stuff, of course, but exactly what residents of the lower forty-eight would expect in a comedy series from the north.

The grizzly bear sequence in episode two was preposterous. The bears were still in their dens at Easter, and no one could get that close without having their head taken off. But, if the audience was willing to suspend their disbelief, he could see the humor.

He straightened the stack of packages that were ready to be handed out to the Board members. Jeffrey's efficient secretary, Bonnie Greenbough, had copied and stapled them together over the past hour.

She seemed delighted to have Jeffrey back. She'd probably be even more delighted when the real Jeffrey arrived and didn't brush off her friendly overtures with excuses about being busy. She seemed like a perfectly nice woman, and Jordan felt guilty avoiding conversations with her.

But he had to keep his head down and his mouth shut, and try not to make any mistakes. There were more people on one floor of the Argonaut office building than in the entire town of Alpine— and they all seemed to know exactly what they were doing. Unlike Jordan, who could barely find the rest room.

He was tiptoeing through a minefield.

His office door opened, and he glanced up, hoping it was Bonnie.

It wasn't.

A drop-dead gorgeous, nattily dressed, perfectly made-up woman strolled through the doorway and snapped the door shut behind her, pausing to lean against it. "Well, well, well," she drawled. "The prodigal returns."

Jordan pushed back in his chair and watched the woman saunter across the large office. "Ashley Baines. In the flesh."

Jeffrey had mentioned her several times.

And Rob had mentioned her too, while pointing out her picture in the company's annual report.

Evidently, the "iron maiden" was Jeffrey's competition for this promotion. Both men had spoken of her with a mixture of awe and fear.

Jordan didn't think she looked all that scary as she folded herself into one of the guest chairs. She arched a perfect brow over glowing blue eyes and gave him a quick, dispassionate once-over.

Scary, no.

Challenging, definitely.

Her crisp, burgundy jacket and the narrow, matching skirt told him she meant business. But her blond braid was like a flash of sunshine in the dark, ostentatious office, and her trim body was the stuff of Jordan's favorite fantasies.

"When did you hit town?" She crossed one leg over the other, showing off tanned, toned calves that held Jordan's attention a little too long.

Maybe that was what scared Jeffrey and Rob so bad. The woman was sexy enough to be lethal.

Good thing Jordan was brave. Good thing he'd taken self-defense training. In fact, he'd be prepared to wrestle her on the carpet if push came to shove.

He'd be prepared to wrestle her at length.

Naked, if necessary.

He dragged his gaze back to her face. "Got in last night," he answered her question.

She zeroed in on the pile of presentations sitting on the wide desk in front of them. Her eyebrows twitched with interest.

He reached out and flipped the papers facedown.

"Scared?" she asked.

He cocked his head to one side. "Of you?"

She laughed at the tone of incredulity, and the sound trickled through him like clear stream water. That laugh sure didn't mesh with the personality Jeffrey had described.

"Of my series," she said.

"We're ready to give you a run for your money." He patted the pile of upside-down papers, considering the merits of locking them in one of the desk drawers until the meeting. Who knew how far she'd go if she happened to stroll into his office and find it empty?

"Can't wait to see it," she said. "But I came to tell you that if you have any tweaking to do, you've caught a break."

"A break?" he asked.

"The meeting's been put off until Friday."

Jordan rocked forward in his chair. Friday? He didn't have until Friday. He'd signed up for *one* day in L.A., not *five* days in L.A. "How the hell did that happen?"

"Stroke of a pen by the chairman of the board's secretary." She looked smug, and a little self-satisfied.
She'd obviously been pivotal in postponing the meeting. But, why? What did she have to gain?

She couldn't know his secret already. Could she?

He gazed into her clear blue eyes for signs that he
was caught.

She stared back, poker-faced, not giving a thing
away.

Jordan had never been any good at mind games. He
much preferred the straight-ahead approach. Like a
wrestling match on the floor of the office—winner got
the promotion.

He wondered if she'd go for it.

"Friday at ten," said Ashley.

"I have an appointment on Friday." In Alpine,
Alaska. Running his company. Wally had only con-
vinced him to do *this* much because he was the closest
thing Jordan had to family.

"So, cancel," she said.

"It's not that simple."

The storm was forecast to last most of the week, so
there was no hope of Jeffrey making it back to save the
day.

Forget the possibility that Jordan would be caught
before Friday, his employees back home were de-
pending on him. The airline wasn't going to run itself.

She smirked, and shrugged her slim shoulders.
"Then don't show. I don't mind."

Then she nodded at the stack of papers, leaning slightly forward in her chair. "I hear yours is set in Alaska."

"*Arctic Luck*," said Jordan, then immediately wondered if he'd made a mistake. Jeffrey had distinctly told him not to share any information with Ashley.

"What's the title?" she asked.

"What's yours?" he returned, not about to get caught out a second time.

She smiled, revealing straight, white teeth and giving those blue eyes a luminescent glow. A shiver of attraction shot to life inside him. He quickly quelled it. That was the *last* thing he needed.

"*Kissed In California*," she replied.

His gaze subconsciously shifted to her full lips. But he quickly blinked his way back to her eyes. Bottomless. Amazingly beautiful.

His brain might know she was off limits, but his libido appreciated what his libido appreciated. There wasn't a whole hell of a lot he could do about it.

"Cute title," he said into the silence.

"It's a cute concept."

"Going to tell me about it?" he asked.

"Not on your life."

"Spoilsport."

"You expect me to make this easy for you?"

"Definitely not."

"Good." She paused. "I'd hate for you to be disappointed."

It was his turn to grin. "I'm not so far."

Her eyes narrowed. "What does that mean?"

"It means I can't wait to see what your medical series is all about."

"Detective series," she corrected.

Jordan's grin widened.

"Don't get all smug on me. I gave you that one."

And she had. He had no doubt.

This was a woman completely in control, completely sure about what she wanted, where she was going and what she was doing.

Jeffrey had her all wrong. She wasn't dangerous. She was intriguing. Sharp and prickly, but definitely intriguing.

"Stop that," she said, eyeing him suspiciously.

"Stop what?"

"Does the bedroom eyes thing actually work in New York?"

"I have no idea what you're talking about."

A challenge glittered in the depths of her irises. "Don't mess with me."

That challenge called to him. It made him envy Jeffrey for getting to work with her all the time. Okay, so Jeffrey got to work *against* her all the time. But it was probably still stimulating as all get out.

She sighed in exasperation and threw up her hands. "What now?"

"You're not what I expected."

"What are you talking about?"

Oops. "I mean, *this* isn't what I expected."

She sat back. "You thought I'd just roll over and play dead as soon as I heard you were showing up?"

Jordan didn't chance answering this time.

She shook her head. "Not on your life, Jeffrey. You just hang on to your New York hat, because I am going to blow you so far out of the East River."

Jordan couldn't help the grin that crept out.

She straightened, and her skirt hiked up showing off an inch of shapely thigh. Her full lips were pursed. And those crystal blue eyes pinned him with a challenge worthy of a wild lynx.

Too bad all that pent-up intensity and emotion was working against him instead of for him. If he ever had a choice, he'd want her on his team. She could probably survive quite nicely in the Alaskan bush.

"Exactly how are you planning to blow me out of the East River?" he asked, wondering if he could fake her into divulging a little more information. Though, if he was honest, he wasn't doing it so much for Jeffrey's sake at this point, as he was trying to best her for the gratification of his own ego.

"With skill and talent," she responded smoothly. "And hard work."

"You don't think *I'm* willing to work hard?"

"I want it more than you do."

"Maybe."

Her eyes widened, and she looked momentarily confused.

Oops. Not a Jeffrey answer. "I mean, I'm sure you *think* you want it more than I do. But, you know me, Ashley—"

"That's right. I do. And I'm not going to let you undermine me this time." She pinned him with a knowing look.

This time? Jordan needed to talk to Jeffrey.

"Then you know I never back away from a fight," he said. That seemed like a safe assumption about Jeffrey. And, it was true enough for Jordan, too.

"Back away?" she scoffed. "I'm sure you'll do your usual end run."

Jordan wasn't sure he liked the sound of that. It made Jeffrey, *him*, sound rather conniving. He was definitely going to find out what Jeffrey had done to this woman.

"I promise you." He looked her straight in the eyes. "Whatever's happened between us in the past, this time you'll see me coming."

See him coming?

What did he mean, see him coming? L.A. studio executives, Jeffrey Bradshaw in particular, were not known for their frontal attacks. Nobody got ahead in this business by giving the competition a chance to mount a defense.

Ashley shut her office door and leaned hard against it, closing her eyes.

What was the matter with her? She'd started off

planning to pump Jeffrey for information, but ended up practically throwing down the gauntlet. Talk about an ill-advised frontal attack. Jeffrey knew more about her plans than she'd ever intended to divulge.

But—she took a deep breath—she hadn't come away completely empty-handed.

She crossed to her desk, adjusted the opaque blinds to block the midday sun from streaming through the picture windows and clicked on her Internet link.

Arctic Luck, Alaska.

"You're slipping, Jeffrey," she muttered to herself.

What was in Arctic Luck, and why would it make a funny television series?

After fifteen minutes of surfing, Ashley had her answer, at least to one of her questions.

Nothing was in Arctic Luck. Nothing at all.

Well, according to the National Forest Service, it had ten unserviced campsites and several miles of grizzly-infested hiking trails. You could catch pike and Arctic grayling in the local lakes—when they weren't frozen solid. And, one of the citizens had made the *Anchorage Daily News* two years ago when his dog team chased off a bull moose during a dogsled race.

As to how Jeffrey planned to make that funny and marketable to a broad demographic, she had absolutely no idea.

Her odd couple/sexy/mismatched buddies/action/fish out-of-water/detective series had to be better than husky dogs and moose. After all, how could a person possibly make a moose sexy?

Not even Jeffrey. Who, well, speaking of sexy...

Ashley closed her eyes again.

Something had happened to Jeffrey while he was away in New York. He suddenly oozed sex appeal. He looked like he'd spent the entire year at the gym and in a tanning booth. She sure didn't remember that rugged, outdoorsy, hardened appearance from last year.

It was distracting. She didn't want to be thinking about his broad shoulders and bulging biceps while she was plotting ways to undermine his bid for the vice presidency. She wanted to focus on his weaknesses and vulnerabilities.

She sat up straight, shaking the mental image, forcing herself to catalogue everything she knew that might be valuable. The series was set in Arctic Luck. It might be a drama, but was probably a comedy, or a combination of both. He hadn't given her the title. But, she'd given him hers.

Damn.

There was nothing in Arctic Luck except wilderness, fish and moose. How was that interesting? How was that funny? He'd hidden his proposal from her, which meant there was something on the front page.

The page.

His proposal was on pages, not on a computer, not in sound bites, not in video clips. He was giving a paper presentation.

There it was. His weakness and her opportunity. If she went flat out—a bells and whistles, high-tech, multimedia extravaganza—she'd win.

Ashley picked up the phone and punched in Rachel's number.

Rachel picked it up on the second ring.

"Did you get Sean Connery?" asked Ashley without preamble.

"No, but I got Greg Duncan for the clips. He's almost as good. Did you pump Jeffrey?"

"I tried." With very limited success. The main thing she'd found out was that there was suddenly something weird about Jeffrey—in an intriguing sexy way. But she wasn't about to share *that* with Rachel.

"What did he tell you?"

"The location. It's Arctic Luck, Alaska."

"Never heard of it."

"That's 'cause you're not a bull moose."

"Huh?"

"Never mind. Little backwater, hole-in-the-wall, near as I can tell. I don't know what Jeffrey's thinking. But, get this, it looks like his presentation is on paper."

"Completely?"

"Uh-huh."

"Maybe they're not as progressive in New York."

"Suits me just fine. Can we film tonight?"

"Got a skeleton crew meeting us at the beach at seven."

ASHLEY AND RACHEL had spent the entire evening filming the first of the new clips. And now Ashley had to stay late that night to layer them into the proposal. That left them with three days before the meeting.

She glanced at her watch. It was nearly three o'clock in the morning. If she worked really fast, she might have time to catch a couple of hours sleep before starting work. She'd let some other things slip yesterday in order to get the filming done, and she'd have to take care of them tomorrow, or rather, later this morning.

She double-clicked the button on the computer in the Argonaut Studios audiovisual computer lab. She was linking still photos, sound bites, video clips and text files into a smooth presentation.

The room held high-end computers with top of the line monitors, specifically designed for video and animation. Argonaut provided them in a central facility for the use of all employees, though the film and photography staff had dibs on them during the day.

The door opened and Ashley turned to see who had joined her. Though official office hours were eight to five, the television industry was a hotbed of last-minute deadlines and emerging crises. No matter what time it was, day or night, there were always a few people working in the main office building.

Her eyes focused on Jeffrey, as he let the door close behind him.

"How's it going?" he asked, in a gravelly voice.

"Fine." She quickly minimized the screen before he could get close enough to see the details.

"A few last-minute adjustments?" he asked, strolling across the dimly lit room.

"A few," she admitted, although it was far more than a few, and she wouldn't consider it last-minute until Thursday night.

"What are *you* doing here?" she asked.

"Just keeping up with the Joneses." He took the computer directly across from her, swiveling the chair to face her. He could have picked any of the other four workstations in the room. The ones farther away from her—out of spying and distracting distance.

"I hear you're setting a high standard." He slid a disk into the drive and began punching keys. "Thanks to you, I'm not getting any sleep tonight."

"Where did you hear that?"

Had he been spying on her? Asking around? Bribing employees? She wouldn't put it past him.

"A gentleman never tells." Jeffrey turned his attention to the computer screen, and she thought she caught a hint of a smile. "We happened to be having dinner on the deck at the Breakwater."

"You just *happened* to be overlooking my shoot?" Ashley didn't believe it for a second. They must have followed her there. The Breakwater deck would have given them a perfect view of last night's filming.

"You were spying on me," she accused.

Jeffrey glanced up. "What do I look like? James Bond?"

No. Actually, he looked more like Daniel Day-Lewis in *The Last of the Mohicans*. With shorter hair and darker eyes. And maybe his chin was stronger, too. Funny, she didn't remember Jeffrey ever looking so rawly sensual.

Wait a minute. Her mind was wandering. What were they talking about?

Spying. Right. She'd lost it there for a moment. Must be sleep deprivation.

She realized his gaze was gaining intensity, and she shifted in her chair. "If you weren't spying on me, what were you doing at the Breakwater?"

"Rob said they had good steaks."

"Since when did you start eating steaks?"

"My third birthday."

"Cute." Maybe that's what bulked up his muscles. Jeffrey had taken to eating red meat over the past year.

He hit a couple of keys on his computer, and a series of colors reflected off the planes and angles of his face.

"You have video clips?" So much for scooping the competition.

"These are stock tourist clips of Alaska. Rob's working with the actors."

Her surprise must have shown on her face.

"You thought I'd just throw in the towel?" he asked softly with a slight shake of his head. "I've got a lot at stake here."

So did she. In fact, so much was at risk here, that even having this conversation was a mistake. She couldn't afford to inadvertently give him any more ammunition against her. She turned her attention to the big monitor in front of her, and enlarged her presentation.

She opened up one of the text files which contained a synopsis on the series idea and started proofreading.

She could hear the clicking of the computer keys as Jeffrey began working.

The overall storyline synopsis looked good, so she moved on to the episode specific stories.

They'd only come up with two episodes so far. They needed at least six.

While she proofread the text in front of her, she let her mind wander to other story ideas.

Before she realized it, she'd stopped reading. As the story ideas rambled through her brain, her action hero sprinted down the beach and suddenly turned into Jeffrey. That made no sense, since Jeffrey was neither old and jaded nor was he gay.

Still, her mind insisted on picturing him tanned and toned against the white sand...with her...in her smallest bikini. She felt the waves tickle her feet and imagined his warm hands on her skin, pausing on the curve of her hip, toying with the ties on her bathing suit.

A shiver of arousal ran through her.

Then the daydream changed. They were in a big

bed. White, gauzy curtains billowed in the ocean breeze through an open window.

She could hear the gulls calling, and the waves crashing. She was in his arms, and it was morning, so they must have made love.

But, darn it, she couldn't remember making love. She stared down at his dark head against the crisp, white pillowcase. She wanted him to wake up so they could make love again.

"Ashley?" His voice was husky against her ear, the soft puff of air erotically tickling her sensitive skin.

He was awake. She turned her head and smiled into his dark, sexy eyes. They were going to make love again, and this time she was going to savor every second.

"You want me to take you home?" he asked.

Home? She shook her head. No way. Not before they made love again.

She tipped her chin, hoping he'd reach out with those big, strong hands and stroke her face.

"Coffee?" he asked. "Or maybe breakfast? It's nearly six."

"Are those my only choices?" she mumbled in the sexiest voice she could muster.

"What other choices do you want?" There was a hint of laughter in his tone.

Ashley was about to tell him in bald terms just exactly what choice she was looking for.

But, suddenly, the hotel room vanished, replaced by

a computer screen. Jeffrey wasn't in her arms in a fantasy bedroom on the oceanfront. He was leaning over her in the Argonaut computer lab.

Icy mortification washed through her. He was waking her up from a catnap and she was about to proposition him.

"Coffee sounds good," she choked out. Coffee. Followed by a long cold shower, and a stern lecture about curbing her fantasy life.

"Want me to bring it here, or you want to go out and grab some breakfast together?"

"What time is it?" She straightened up in the padded chair.

"Nearly six," he said.

She lifted her hand to her forehead, combing back the fine hairs which had worked their way loose from her braid. Checking her skirt and short-sleeved sweater she made sure everything was in the right place.

Two hours? She'd been asleep for two hours?

As the implication sunk in, her gaze flew to her computer screen. He could have done *anything* in two hours. He could have read her whole presentation. He could have erased it or sabotaged it.

"The answer is nothing," he said dryly.

"I didn't say a word."

"It's written all over your face." He straightened. "I'm an honest man, Ashley. I want to win, but not at the cost of my principles."

Principles? Ashley blinked. That wasn't a word bandied about in the L.A. television industry very often.

She honestly didn't know whether to believe him or not.

"Besides, if I betrayed you while you slept, there's nothing you can do about it now. Let me buy you some bacon and eggs."

"I don't eat meat."

"Then, let me buy you pancakes and fruit. Not to brag or anything, but you're going to need your strength if you're going up against me."

As Ashley stared into his eyes, the sensations from the dream burst back through her mind, making her shiver with the memory. She'd felt so safe in his arms. More safe and loved and cherished than she'd ever imagined possible.

"You okay?" he asked.

She nodded, squeezing her eyes shut, reality warring with fantasy.

"Come on, sleepyhead." He slipped an arm around her shoulders, strong fingers coaxing her up. His voice was a sensual rumble near her ear. "Let's get you something to eat."

Ashley yielded to the pressure of his arm. Yielded to the magic of her dream. Yielded to the charisma of the new Jeffrey. She allowed him to draw her into a standing position, her body brushing his broad chest.

Had he grown taller?

No. That was silly.

"When's the last time you slept?" he asked, voice soft.

She shrugged her shoulders, making no move to pull away. "What day is this?" She gave a quick, nervous laugh.

He cocked his head, looking deep into her eyes for a long moment. Then something subtly shifted in his expression, and he quickly blinked.

His fingertips held her arm a little more tightly. "Uh. You better let me take you home to bed."

Ashley drew a quick breath, her breasts brushing against him for a split second.

He didn't mean...

Of course he didn't mean that.

But, she had *such* a craving.

"Ashley?" He sighed her name, and his gaze darkened.

"Jeffrey?" she whispered back, subconsciously leaning in.

Just one little kiss. She just wanted a sample. Just a taste of what she'd missed in her dream.

His arm slipped to her waist and tightened around her. He shook his head and muttered something under his breath. Then he drew her cheek against the thin fabric of his dress shirt, rocking ever so slightly.

Something inside her shuddered, then settled, then sighed.

"This is bad," he whispered against her hair, voice sounding strained.

He stroked his palm down her disheveled braid. His chest rose and fell with several deep breaths.

"Yeah," she agreed, as the heat of his hand seeped into every single follicle.

"I cannot believe..."

She waited, but he didn't finish the sentence. She tipped her head back so she could look him in the eyes. Her lips softened and her knees grew weak.

This was bad, but in *such* a good way.

3

JORDAN GAZED down at Ashley's slumberous eyes and inviting lips, soft and deep pink in the flickering light from her computer screen. On second thought, bad was an understatement.

This was a disaster.

He knew he had to walk away—now, before things got out of hand. But somehow, he couldn't get that message to his legs.

She blinked her long lashes. Once, then twice, then three times. She looked slightly tousled from sleep—that crisp, perfect, don't-touch-me edge gone.

Desire convulsed within him.

He stroked his fingertips over her hair, reveling in its soft texture, inhaling the subtle scent of her wildflower perfume. "Do you think..."

"Yes?" she answered on a whisper, her sweet breath puffing against his skin.

His hand tightened involuntarily around the rope of her braid. "That if I kissed you..."

Her eyes closed, and she softened in his arms.

He moved another inch and brushed his lips gently

across hers, testing the tender skin, absorbing the heat. "That in two minutes..."

A small shudder ran through her.

"Maybe five minutes..." he amended, pausing, puckering, holding her moist lips for a single heart-beat.

Her hands came up to grip his biceps.

He touched her lower lip with the tip of his tongue and sensation rocketed to his toes. "In, say, ten minutes from now... We could walk out of here and forget it ever happened?"

"Jeffrey?" Her voice was small. Her fingertips dug into his arms, bringing far more pleasure than pain.

"Yeah?" he breathed.

"You're already kissing me."

"Oh, no, I'm not." He shook his head. This wasn't kissing.

But if she was willing...

He gave her a second to pull away. Then he opened his mouth, tipped his head, captured her lips, and sealed them together in a fusion of heat and pent-up passion, his brain blinded to everything but the feel and taste of Ashley.

She came up on her toes, and he settled his arm more firmly around her waist, pulling her tight against his tension-filled body. His fingers tangled in her hair, thumb stroking her cheek, circling her ear, dipping, delving, finding the tender, secret places on the back of her neck.

He flicked his tongue against the inside of her lips, and her mouth opened wider on a moan. Her hands slid to his shoulders and she held on, tipping her head to one side. Her tongue met his halfway, tangling in a burst of heated need.

Now *this* was kissing.

His fingertips found the silky skin between her short sweater and her little skirt, twitching in reaction. He longed to explore further, but they'd only agreed on a kiss.

So, he focused on her mouth, kissing her longer, harder, deeper. Coming up for air to pepper the corners of her mouth with mini kisses, tasting her soft skin, inhaling the hidden scent where her neck curved into her shoulder.

And then he was back to her mouth, because that was the apex of her magic. The computers hummed in the background, the multicolored screens bathing the room in a soft glow. Jordan was losing his center, losing his perspective.

She tasted of sweet coffee and midnight dreams, and he wanted the kiss to go on forever.

But the kiss was a lie.

He was living a lie.

She thought he was Jeffrey, and Jeffrey thought she was the enemy. And here in L.A., Jordan Adamson didn't even exist. Of all the off-limits women in the whole off-limits world, Ashley took first prize.

There was no way for this to turn out well.

Though his body screamed for mercy, Jordan loosened his hold. He forced his hand to let go of her hair. He broke from her lips, gathering his strength, steeling his desire, then going back for a single, lightning-fast kiss of regret.

Her eyes flickered open. A deep breath slipped out between her swollen lips.

"Our ten minutes are up," he whispered, touching his forehead to hers.

"So soon?" she asked.

Not a moment too soon, his brain pointed out. Even though his body strongly disagreed.

"You okay?" he asked. He was okay. Well, except for the fact that the universe had just shifted and he was struggling to get his bearings.

"That was..." She took a step back, slipping from his arms, breaking their touch.

"Cataclysmic?" It wasn't the perfect word. But he didn't think the perfect word existed to describe what had just happened between them.

She squared her shoulders, the tough, professional Ashley emerging from the soft, romantic goddess. "A *really* big mistake."

She was right, but it pricked his pride. He wasn't about to let her shift gears that quickly. "You didn't like it?" he asked.

"Quit fishing."

Jordan gave her a cocky half smile, hoping to shake

a reaction out of her. "I don't need another compliment. Your actions speak louder than words."

"What actions?"

"You kissed me. Seriously."

She gave a light laugh, and smoothed her hair back, her expression going neutral. She might have been staring at a log sheet for all the emotion in her eyes. "I don't know what you're talking about."

Jordan was taken aback by the complete transformation. "Are you telling me I imagined your reaction?"

No way. Not a chance. A woman couldn't fake that.

She smiled smugly. "This is Hollywood, Jeffrey." She reached past him to pop her disk out of the computer. "Everything's an illusion." Then she straightened and saluted him with the plastic cover. "See you at the Board meeting on Friday."

Jordan watched the sway of her hips as she walked out the door.

Acting?

If she could act like that, the woman deserved an award.

Of course, this *was* L.A. And she *was* in the television business. Who was to say she didn't start out as an actress?

Still.

He'd bet she wasn't that good.

And, he'd bet that if they kissed again, he could prove it. He squared his shoulders. If he met her in her office, or in his office, or in one of the 26th floor meet-ing rooms...

One more chance, and he could show her who was and wasn't acting.

Yeah.

He nodded his head.

Then he shook his head.

What was he thinking? He might be leaving on Fri-day, but Jeffrey was coming back to stay. The man had to work for Argonaut Studios. He had to work with Ashley. Jordan couldn't leave a disaster in his wake.

SOMEBODY UP THERE was out to get Ashley.

Her heels clicked on the hallway floor as she made her way toward the east wing of the studio at three in the afternoon.

When Harold Gauthier, the chairman of the board, had asked her to attend tonight's Platinum party at his mansion, she'd been overjoyed. It was an A-list party, a sure sign she was being noticed in the upper eche-lons of the studio.

In the split second after he'd issued the invitation, she'd planned her wardrobe, her hair, even pondered if she'd have time for a quick facial and a pedicure.

But then he'd dropped the bombshell.

"Get Jeffrey Bradshaw to pick you up," he'd said.

And, of course, she'd said, "love it." And suddenly, instead of going to the party as an up-and-coming executive, she was going to the party as the *date* of an up-and-coming executive.

For a minute there, Harold had actually reminded her of her father. And that chafed.

What was *with* men?

Why couldn't they simply see her as a professional? Not a *female* professional, but simply a colleague.

Her father was wonderful, and she loved him dearly, but he had an annoying habit of trying to second-guess her life. With the best of intentions, he kept asking why she was knocking herself out to get ahead in her career, since she'd probably meet a good man and quit anyway.

Her brothers were the same way, mired somewhere in 1950s thinking. And the one and only time she'd been in a serious relationship, the man squashed her professional aspirations so fast she'd barely known what hit her.

"There's nothing wrong with a career, darling." Reggie had said as her three-carat diamond solitaire sparkled hypnotically in the candlelight at Ruffino's. "It just has to be the right career. You know, maybe something at the museum or the gallery, a hostess, part-time. At least until the children come along. You've got all the right clothes."

Actually, she hadn't had all the right clothes.

Thank goodness.

She had power clothes. He'd wanted low-key elegance followed by designer-maternity and upscale-housewife.

Ashley definitely did *not* have the right clothes to marry Reggie Lawrence.

She approached Jeffrey's office and took a deep breath, bracing herself to take him on next.

Men.

When they weren't trying to marry you off, they were throwing themselves in your career path.

"Is he in, Bonnie?" she asked his secretary.

Bonnie glanced at the buttons on her phone. "Go ahead. He just finished a call."

Ashley twisted the doorknob and breezed inside. No point in letting him think that kiss this morning had been more than passing curiosity. No point in letting him think she was anything less than thrilled about taking him to the party. And no point in letting him know that she was ready to scream at the prospect of her gender getting in the way of business, yet again.

"Busy tonight?" she asked, hoping against hope he'd say yes and she could be on her way to the salon, then go to the party alone.

Jeffrey cocked his head to one side, a smile playing on his lips. "Why?" he drawled. "You got something in mind?"

Despite herself, her heart skipped a little beat before she could squelch the reaction. She immediately ordered herself to stop. Jeffrey had been messing with her head this morning.

No doubt those sweet words and that over-the-top kiss were part of some scheme or other he'd cooked up. Well, she wasn't falling for it. So there.

"Don't flatter yourself," she said. "Harold Gauthier invited us to the Platinum party."

She paused and waited for his response.

His expression tightened. "You mean with studio people?"

What was the matter with him? He didn't look thrilled at the prospect of the party, he looked worried.

"Of course with studio people. It's for *Paradise Island.*" She paused again. "You remember? The theme song went platinum last week. It was in all the papers."

"I guess they didn't cover it in Alaska."

"You didn't have the trades couriered up?" Ashley had a sudden urge to put her hand on his forehead and check for a fever.

He stood up from his desk, and came around to stand in front of her. "I was out in the bush for a while. Out of touch. That's great. Of course I'll come."

Of course he'd come, in that bored, blasé voice? Forget the fever, maybe she should check for a pulse.

She tilted her head to look into his eyes. They were softer, more brown than she remembered. And there were creases in their corners, as if he'd laughed a lot in New York.

He had a five-o'clock shadow, though it was only three. And there was a new scar on his chin. A little thing, but one that made her think he had secrets.

And his lips. Suddenly, the sensation of his lips on hers bloomed in her mind—that first touch, the tender nonkiss that had curled her toes, and then the mind-bending, sensually exquisite kisses that followed.

Only eight hours ago, his lips had been on hers.

Everything between them was the same. And yet everything had changed.

She suddenly needed a touchstone of their former relationship. "You remember the *Galactic Warrior* party?" she asked.

He hesitated for just a split second. "Sure."

"The blue Jell-O and Sweetarts?"

"Who could forget." He paused again, and his eyebrows quirked. "I seem to recall you had too much champagne that night."

Ashley smiled, and something inside her relaxed. This was better. Her uptight Jeffrey was back. "You obviously remember the pool incident."

"It *was* pretty funny."

"Easy for you to say. You didn't end up looking like the winner of a wet T-shirt contest."

A muscle in his cheek twitched, and his gaze dropped to her breasts, obviously zeroing in on the memory.

"Men are pigs," she said.

"We're just honest."

"No. You're swine."

"We can't help it."

"Try."

"Yes, ma'am."

"You learn that in New York?"

"What?"

"Say it again."

His brow creased in puzzlement.

"Yes, ma'am," she repeated. "I like the sound of it. I think you should practice it. I think you should start saying that every time I ask you something."

Jeffrey smirked. "Yes, ma'am."

She rubbed her hands together. "Oh. This is good. Pick me up at eight."

"Yes, ma'am?"

"Bring me flowers?"

He took a step closer, and his voice dropped an octave, his words slowed down. "Yes, ma'am."

She shivered at the sound. "Candy?"

He leaned in. "Yes, ma'am."

She inhaled his clean, earthy scent, and her heart rate doubled. Her gaze dropped to his lips.

"Yes, ma'am," he whispered, guessing her thoughts, tilting his head.

No, sir. She ducked out of the way, heading for the door. "Eight o'clock. My place," she tossed over her shoulder.

A WARM BREEZE blew across Jordan's face, and the palm trees on Malibu Boulevard swayed in the tangy ocean breeze. He and Ashley sat silently, waiting on another red light. Music from the clubs and aromas from the open air restaurants combined in an exotic mixture of sensation.

The light turned green and he pushed on the accelerator of Jeffrey's red convertible, pulling the gearshift into second as he gained speed along the smooth pavement. Hard to believe he'd been digging his way out of a snowbank only two days ago.

Though he was born in Seattle, his parents had adopted him as an infant, and he'd spent his whole life in Alaska, never experiencing a warm summer night.

A guy could sure get used to this.

As he settled into third, he stretched his arm out across the back of the bench seat, almost, but not quite touching Ashley's bare shoulder. Her hair was loose and blowing in the breeze. Her eyes were closed, her head tipped back, and her hand made swimming motions in the air currents beside the car.

He had known he'd dressed all wrong by the way she'd stared at his suit when he picked her up. And her bright orange sarong and bikini top were a giveaway of the party dress code.

Paradise Island. It fit.

She fit.

She looked great sitting there beside him.

He had a sudden urge to forget all about the party and drive forever into the warm night. Maybe they could head up the coast, find a nice quiet beach and go swimming or skinny-dipping. Or just make love on the sand.

"You want to make a deal?" she asked, opening her eyes and straightening in her seat. Her hand dropped down into her lap, and his momentary vision of the soft Ashley was gone.

So much for making love on the sand. He was pretty sure that wasn't what she was about to offer.

"Depends," he answered slowly, not quite ready to let go of his fantasy.

"On what?"

"Does it involve kissing you again?"

Her spine straightened even more. "Of course not."

"Why not?"

"Be serious. Here's the deal. You stay out of my way tonight, and I'll stay out of your way. We both know what an opportunity this is. No reason we both can't take advantage of it."

Jordan didn't particularly like the sound of that deal. He was sure Jeffrey would know what to do at the party, but he didn't have a clue.

Besides, it seemed like a crying shame to show up with a woman this stunning and then ditch her.

"I thought we could dance," he said.

She laughed. "What on earth for?"

"Because that's what people do at parties. And because we're attracted to each other."

"Speak for yourself."

"Uh-uh." He shook his head and let his fingertips graze the tip of her shoulder. "You're not getting away with that. You know you are."

She flinched from his touch. "You have an ego the size of Texas."

"The size of Alaska. It's much bigger than Texas. But that doesn't mean I'm wrong."

"You are most definitely wrong."

"Prove it."

"How?"

"Kiss me again and don't react."

"I already did that once."

"Like hell."

"I told you I was acting. Didn't feel a thing."

He slowed down for another light. "You lie."

"You dream."

"Shall I pull over and prove it now, or do you want to try again at the party?"

"Neither," she said tartly. "You keep your hands on the wheel and your eyes on the road."

"Yes, ma'am."

"And, at the party, you're on your own so I can schmooze with Harold Gauthier."

"You're big on schmoozing, aren't you?"

"What do you mean?"

Jordan glanced at her for a second. "You think it'll help your chances for the promotion?"

"Of course."

"So, you think he'll promote style over substance?" It seemed like a ridiculous way to run a company.

"Who says you've got more substance than me?" Ashley crossed her arms over her bikini top, pushing her breasts up against the fabric.

"Not a soul," said Jordan, holding up a palm to protest his innocence, his attention bouncing between the road and her cleavage.

"That was a veiled insult if I ever heard one," she said.

"There was nothing *veiled* in any of that. I asked if he'd hire style over substance, and that's exactly what I wanted to know."

"No. You insinuated that you have more substance than me, and the only way I'll get the job is by vamping the boss. What is *with* you men?"

"What men? Hey, I'm the only guy in the car."

"You're all alike."

"Oh, well, that was a rational argument."

A small smirk crept through her irritation. "It's been scientifically proven."

"Right. I remember an MIT study done in 1985. We're all swine."

"Exactly."

"Odd then, that you like kissing me so much."

"I don't."

"You did this morning,"

"I was acting," Ashley repeated without missing a beat.

"Prove it."

Her mouth tightened as she fought the smile. "Nice try. But you won't goad me into kissing you."

"Can I guilt you into kissing me?"

She shook her head determinedly. "No."

"Bribe you?"

"No way."

"Seduce you?"

"Not a chance."

"I give up. You tell me how to do it."

"You're amazing."

"Let me show you the ways."

Ashley nodded to a lantern-topped brick pillar. "There's the driveway."

Jordan quickly turned his attention back to the road and pulled the convertible into a tree-lined, semicircular driveway. It was made of exposed aggregate rock, and two lighted pillars guarded the entrance.

As they rounded the bend, a lush lawn appeared, and the sounds of a steel drum band filled the air. Backlit by floodlights from a waterfall fountain, hula dancers gyrated to the music.

He pulled to a stop next to a valet who was dressed like a surfer, and gave the man the keys.

Then he rounded the front of the car and offered his hand to Ashley.

To his surprise, she took it and held her sarong carefully as she rose from the seat. But she drew away as soon as they started up the wide, marble staircase.

"Good evening, Mr. Bradshaw," said a gentleman at the front door. His English accent was decidedly at odds with his loud shirt and string sandals. Jordan was beginning to feel out of place in his suit.

"Good evening," he returned, trying his best to sound like Jeffrey.

"Ms. Baines," he said to Ashley.

Then he looked at Jordan again. "Through the atrium, and out onto the deck. You know the way." He gestured them inside with an outstretched hand.

"Sure," said Jordan, glancing surreptitiously around the entry, trying to decide if he should head down the hallway, or along the row of windows and marble pillars.

He slowed until another guest passed them, and then he followed to where several glass French doors appeared, leading onto a wide balcony.

He whistled under his breath as he took in the expanse of beach, pool deck and manicured lawn. There was definitely a lot of money around Jeffrey's life.

They stepped through the doorway, just as a loud boom pierced the night air. Jordan's stomach clenched as a twenty-foot, orange inferno shot out from a cluster of tropical plants toward the dark sky.

He instinctively grabbed Ashley around the waist,

pulling her back into the house. "The garden's on fire," he whispered hoarsely.

He glanced around, trying to figure out where she'd be safest.

"It's the *volcano*." She stared up at him in amazement as she recovered her balance.

He stared back, trying to figure out what the hell she was talking about.

"You know," she continued, "the Mauna Launa from special effects?"

"Of course." He relaxed his hold on her waist, willing his pulse rate to return to normal. "I forgot about that. They don't have them in New York."

He quickly glanced away from her, turning his attention back to the big yard, trying to get his bearings. He catalogued a buffet decorated with ice sculptures, a tiki torch pathway leading to the beach, a side of pork roasting on an open spit and a small band on a central gazebo.

Nothing else looked ready to explode. Thank goodness.

"You look like you could use a Pele's Passion," said Ashley.

Hoping that Pele's Passion was a drink, Jordan nodded. "I see a bar over by the pool. Want me to get you one, too?"

"Trying to get me drunk so I can't schmooze properly?"

Jordan knew he should resist a comeback. He

should leave her alone, wander around, blend in with the crowd, listen in on a few Hollywood conversations.

If nothing else, the folks back in Alpine would get a kick out of some real Hollywood gossip.

That's what he *should* do.

But he couldn't resist the challenge of Ashley. And, despite her protests, she had *flirt with me,* written all over her face. "I'm trying to get you drunk so you'll dance with me."

"Is being nice to me some kind of strategy to keep me from fighting dirty?"

Jordan grinned. "Oh, no. I want you to fight dirty."

She rolled her eyes. "Give it a rest."

"Okay. Here's the deal. One drink, one dance, and I guarantee you'll *want* to kiss me. After that, I'll leave you alone to schmooze."

"And if I *don't* want to kiss you?"

He shrugged. "No guts, no glory."

She pushed her loose hair behind her ears. "I have no idea what that meant."

"It meant, I'm a risk-taking kind of guy."

"That's why you're going for a Pele's Passion? After all these years?"

"Bring it on."

"Photograph, sir?" A man with a camera in his hand, held out a Polaroid of Jordan and Ashley deep in conversation. She looked saucy, and he looked

amused. He knew it was a moment he wanted to remember.

"Sure." He took the picture and pulled out his wallet. "How much do I owe you?"

"They're complimentary," said the man.

"Oh." He hesitated, wallet open.

"Tip," Ashley muttered in his ear.

Of course. How much did a person tip for this?

He quirked an eyebrow in Ashley's direction.

She reached into his wallet and pulled out a ten dol-
lar bill, handing it to the photographer.

"Couldn't remember what was standard," said Jordan weakly.

"Did they by any chance give you shock therapy in
New York?"

"I think it must have been the hallucinogenic
drugs."

"Really?" She drew back.

"Of course not."

"But you're willing to try a Pele's Passion."

"Is it a hallucinogenic drug?"

"Closest thing to it that's legal."

"This I have got to try."

They headed directly for the large bar. A waterfall
pool twinkled just below them in the reflection of the
tiki torches.

"There's Gregory Simpson," whispered Ashley,
pressing against Jordan's arm while she spoke in
his ear.

"I see," Jordan nodded. Pretending he had the slightest idea who she was talking about.

"You want to stop and say hi?"

"You go ahead. I'll order the drinks."

"You sure?"

"I'm sure."

Ashley gave him a quick squeeze on the arm, and glided over to two men who were standing next to the pool.

They smiled warmly as she approached and reached out to shake her hand. Who wouldn't? One of them said something to her, which was obviously about her outfit, because she stepped back and struck a pose, an engaging smile on her face.

Jordan dragged his gaze away and headed the rest of the way to the bar.

He waited a few minutes for the bartender to finish another order, then he asked for two Pele's Passions.

"Thanks," said Ashley breathlessly, coming up beside him. "That went great."

"I'm glad," he said.

"You've changed."

"Two Pele's Passions," said the bartender, handing them two hollowed out pineapples with fruit kabobs, double straws and little blue paper umbrellas.

They each took one of the drinks.

Jordan leaned over near Ashley's ear. "Tip?" he asked in an undertone.

"Optional," she replied.

Jordan handed the man a ten.

He heard a fizzing sound and glanced down at the ornate drinks. They were foaming up like volcanoes, and he reached out to grab Ashley's, getting it out of her hand just as the sticky liquid overflowed.

"Thanks," she smiled.

"My granddaddy always taught me to come to the aid of a lady in distress." He glanced at the receding drinks. "I think they should rename these Pele's Revenge."

Jordan wiped the outside of her pineapple with a cocktail napkin and handed the drink back to her as they moved away from the bar.

"What should we drink to?" she asked, coming to a halt beneath a palm tree at the edge of the lawn and turning to face him. The moonlit beach was at her back, and the light from a tiki torch flickered on her face.

Her sunshine-blond hair bounced softly around her smooth shoulders. Her long lashes looked like something out of a magazine ad, and her teeth were gleaming white and perfectly straight. She had the kind of flawless beauty a man only dreamed about.

"Moonlight kisses?" he asked.

"Ever the optimist," she smiled.

"It's part of my charm."

"Funny that I never noticed it before."

"My optimism?"

"Your charm."

Jordan felt a grin growing on his face. "You're admitting I have charm."

She pursed her lush lips, sapphire eyes squinting. "It's the strangest thing...."

Jordan realized she was wandering into dangerous territory. He sure didn't want her thinking too hard about how much he'd changed since she last saw Jeffrey.

"How about we drink to the new vice president." He raised his pineapple.

"Whoever that may be?" said Ashley.

"May the better...uh, person win." He touched his pineapple to hers and took a sip of the drink through one of the straws.

The sweet tangy fruit taste exploded into an alcoholic volcano as it made its way down his throat. He suppressed a coughing reflex.

Ashley wasn't as successful. She coughed deep in her throat, tears making her eyes glisten. "I'm not sure this was such a good idea," she wheezed. "Not if we want to schmooze coherently."

"Lightweight," he teased.

"Definitely."

"Oh, good. What can we drink to next?"

"How about your birthday?"

Jordan froze. "My *what*?"

"Happy birthday." She held up her drink.

The implication of her words slammed Jordan in the gut with the force of a two-by-four. It *was* his birthday.

But, Ashley couldn't know that.
She had to be talking about Jeffrey's birthday.
Which meant.
No way. No how.
He scrambled for Jeffrey's wallet.

4

"IS SOMETHING WRONG?" asked Ashley.

Jeffrey's expression had gone from teasing to shocked in the blink of an eye. He slowly set his drink down on one of the patio tables, and stared at his open wallet like he'd seen a ghost.

She moved a little closer, trying to figure out what had upset him. "Did you lose something?"

He flipped the wallet closed, held it tight in his fist, and shook his head. "No. I just..." He glanced around at the party. "Do you mind if I take off?"

Take off? Why on earth would he cut out on the party of the year? "You're *leaving*?"

"I just need to get some air. I'll be back in plenty of time to drive you home."

"It's not that—"

"I'm really sorry." He pivoted on the heel of his loafer and headed for the beach.

"Jeffrey?" she called after him. What had just happened? What had she missed?

One minute they were joking, and the next he couldn't wait to get away from her.

She watched his retreating back as he paced toward

the sandy shoreline. When he came to the surf, he turned north, away from her, away from the torch-light of the party.

The wind rustled his short hair, and his shoes left prints in the soft, wet sand.

She stood there for a minute, not sure whether to be annoyed or relieved. First he was a jerk. Then he was a flirt. And now he was blowing her off?

What on earth was the matter with him?

While she tried to decide what his problem might be, bass notes began to throb from the speakers behind her, telling her the dancing was about to start.

Glasses clinked, voices rose and fell with hypnotic regularity and laughter flitted through the palm trees.

Ashley turned her attention to the guests who were milling around the pool and chatting over the buffet and the bar. The party was well underway, and it was time for her to get to work.

She set her drink down next to Jeffrey's, running her fingertips through her loose hair. Then she pulled a mirror and lipstick out of her clutch purse and did a quick repair.

If Jeffrey wanted to leave the field clear for her, that was totally up to him. It was none of her business if he decided on a sudden stroll down the beach. It was nothing to do with her at all.

It was time to see and be seen.

Still, she couldn't help one last, quick glance. His business suit looked out of place on the beach. And he looked strangely lonely as he faded into the blue-black night.

Something clenched inside her.

What if the problem was serious?

What if he needed her? They weren't exactly friends, but they weren't strangers either. Maybe something terrible had happened.

Then she stopped herself.

But what if it wasn't serious?

What if he'd just turned strange in New York?

What if she screwed up the party of the year over nothing?

Damn.

She gazed longingly at the party guests, the Gauthiers, the Simpsons, the Cunninghams. Then she sighed in resignation, stripped off her sandals and trotted after Jeffrey.

The sand was deep and soft, still slightly warm from the late-day sunshine. Her bare feet sank into it with every pace, making jogging many times harder as Jeffrey's long strides took them farther down the shoreline toward a deserted stretch of beach.

The terrain changed, and cliffs rose up beside her.

"Jeffrey?" she gasped when she got within range. "Jeffrey?"

He turned. His brows furrowed together in the moonlight. "Ashley?"

"What's going on?" She came to a halt beside him, lungs laboring as she struggled to catch her breath.

"What are you doing?" he asked.

"I'm out jogging."

At his look of confusion, she rolled her eyes. "What do you think I'm doing? I came to see what was wrong with you."

"You shouldn't have done that. Go back to the party and do that schmoozy thing you keep talking about."

"I'm not leaving you like this."

"I'm fine."

"No, you're not."

He didn't answer.

His expression went enigmatic again, and he turned away, his eyes focusing on the dark, rolling water. The silence stretched between them. The incoming tide lapped onto the shore, and the cold water nipped at Ashley's bare feet.

"It's nothing," he finally said.

"You're lying," she countered, studying the tightness in his jaw.

The tension within him was palpable. His shoulders were rigid. His muscles bunched with restrained energy. She'd never seen him look so wild, so untouchable, so very far away.

She knew she should leave him alone. Their relationship might be shifting, but she'd offered her help, and he'd said no. It was exactly what she should have expected. A drink and a couple of laughs did not make a friendship.

Whatever was going on in his life, he obviously didn't need or want her help.

Then, suddenly, without interrupting his intense study of the stars on the far horizon, he muttered, "You're right."

She was right?

And he'd admitted it?

He drew in a slow breath, and gripped the corded muscles at the back of his neck.

He needed comfort. He'd never ask for it, but she knew deep down inside that he was desperate for it at that moment.

Taking a deep breath of her own, she placed her palm lightly on his shoulder. His suit jacket was cool under her fingers. And she could feel his steel-hard muscles beneath the fabric.

"So, what is it?" she asked.

He shifted his gaze to her hand, staring at it for a long moment as the incoming tide surged across the beach. Then he reached up and covered her fingers with his own, squeezing gently. "I really wish I could tell you."

His hand was warm. It was rough. It was strong, and pulsating with life.

"That's okay," she whispered, taking the small step closer, trying to comfort without being demanding. He reminded her of the classic tough guy. Solid and stoic on the outside, but vulnerable at the most unexpected moments.

"Is it really bad?" she asked softly.

He shook his head, lifting her hand to brush her knuckles against his cheek.

She took the gesture as an invitation, turning her hand, cupping his face, skimming her fingertips across his rough skin. An intimacy arced between them, surpassing even their kisses.

He snaked his arm around the small of her back, and his fingers settled against her bare skin. He tightened his hold, urging her closer. "As a matter of fact, it's pretty good."

"Yeah?" She tipped her head and looked into his eyes, offering a small, relieved smile.

He held her gaze, releasing her hand to brush his fingertips against her cheek. "Scary as hell…"

She leaned into his touch, and a glow of awareness rose softly within her. Her knees started to weaken as the magic returned. She remembered his touch, his scent, the sound of his voice reverberating through her body.

"Scary as hell, but in a good way?" she asked, secretly reliving those moments she'd spent in his arms.

"You've got it," he answered.

She stared into his soft, dark eyes, trying to guess what he was thinking. It was impossible.

But she knew exactly what *she* was thinking. And it wasn't about offering comfort anymore. Her thoughts had turned selfishly sensual.

The ocean breeze rustled her skirt, teasing her bare legs. Every nerve ending in her body came to life.

She tunneled her fingers into his hairline, tipping her head farther into the palm of his hand, bringing her chin up in an invitation that had to be pretty hard to mistake. "Some things are like that," she whispered.

"Oh, yeah," he breathed. "Some things are definitely like that."

The hand on her bare back splayed and tightened, and his fingertips pushed into her hair, brushing her earlobe, cupping the back of her neck, drawing her forward.

He tipped his head counterpoint, dipping, touching his lips to hers.

They were warm and gentle, sweet from Pele's Passion.

Then he drew her flush against him, and his mouth opened wider. His kisses changed from light and teasing to firm and serious. The tip of his tongue flicked out, moistening her lips, testing the texture of her mouth.

The waves burbled around her toes, and the stars winked against the midnight-purple sky, blurring as her lids fluttered closed.

As the kiss went on, surges of water poured restlessly around her ankles, pushing her one way, then pulling her the other. She lost her balance as sand swirled from beneath her feet.

She wrapped her arms around Jeffrey, anchoring herself to his sturdy body.

He encircled her waist, lifting her slightly. Then he repositioned his mouth so that it fused to hers, heat on heat as the cool ocean waves caressed her. His tongue plunged inside her mouth, and she thought she might explode from pure sensation. His fingertips were strong and callused and erotic, and a moan broke free from her lips.

"Scared?" he breathed against her mouth.

"In a good way," she breathed back.

It was so good. So incredibly, unbelievably good.

He kissed her again, openmouthed, hard and determined, drawing out her passion.

Then his fingertips skimmed their way down her rib cage, across her hip bone, kneading over the curve of her buttocks. The touch seared straight through the thin fabric of her sarong.

When he stroked the back of her thighs, her muscles contracted, her lungs filling with the deepest of breaths. Her pulse rate sped up. Heat rushed through her body, drenching her skin in a fine sweat.

His hands fisted the fabric of her skirt, drawing it up the backs of her legs in a slow, sensual torture.

He kissed her neck. She tipped her head back and gave him free access, biting down on her bottom lip as her toes curled into the wet sand.

She tugged his suit jacket off his shoulders, and he impatiently tossed it aside.

His tongue found the pulse point at the base of her collarbone, and his hand stroked up the side of her rib cage, his thumb butterflying beneath one breast. Her nipples instantly beaded beneath the bikini top, and she moved his hand to cup her.

"You're gorgeous," he whispered.

"You're amazing," she whispered back.

And then he was kissing her again, hot heavy kisses that drew every ounce of longing from her body. She met his tongue full-on. His thumb and index finger tightened on her nipple, and shock waves ricocheted between her thighs.

"I want you," he rasped. "So bad."

"Oh, yeah." She tore at his shirt buttons, desperate to feel his skin against hers.

His hands trailed down her back in answer, releasing her bikini top, freeing her breasts to the night air.

He got rid of his own shirt, and gathered her against him. Skin on skin, finally.

She kneaded her fingertips into his muscles, exploring every inch of his shoulders, his biceps, his chest, reveling in his strength.

He backed them into the shelter of a rock formation, then released the knot on her sarong. He spread his legs, pulling her tight into the vee. She pushed against his straining erection, feeling every single sensation through her whisper-thin panties.

He bent to take her nipple in his mouth.

Desire clawed at her as his rough tongue molded

and stroked and shaped her flesh. She fumbled with his zipper, writhing against his hardened body, desperate to get closer.

He bent his knees, drawing her down with him, laying back on the sand and setting her astride his hard stomach while he tugged off his pants.

His washboard stomach was hot against her moist flesh.

Watching him in awe, she dragged the tangy air into her laboring lungs. The surf surged on, and the moon broke free of the hills.

They were naked, tangled, aroused, and Ashley could barely believe it was happening.

He stilled, and stared into her eyes for a long second, brushing a wayward wisp of hair from her cheek. Then cupped her face, pulling her slowly down to meet his lips.

As their tongues tangled, he ran his palms down her back, over her buttocks, along her thighs, slipping in between, stretching, invading, sending a heated pulse all the way to her toes. Her knees dug into the soft, grainy sand, and she shimmied down his body, shamelessly seeking his hardness and heat.

He settled his big hands around her hips. "Now?" he asked.

"Now," she nodded.

He stared into her eyes as he pressed her hips down, levering himself up, stretching her, filling her, urging her up tight against him.

When he was in, solid, he stopped. They both held their breath. The surf pounded faster, and the wind picked up, swirling the thick, moisture-laden air around their heated bodies.

He took her hands, lacing his fingers with hers, holding tight, jaw clenched.

She shifted her hips, but he shook his head no.

"Stay still," he hissed in a strained whisper. "For as long as you can."

Ashley gritted her teeth as sensation swelled between her legs. Her body screamed for movement, screamed for release. Her knees tightened against his sides.

"Kiss me," he said.

She bent, opened her mouth and curled her tongue around his. She resolutely held her hips still and put all her intense, yearning emotions into the kiss.

When she finally pulled back, his eyes were glazed.

"Now?" she asked, voice strained.

"Not—" He took a couple of labored breaths. *"Yes!"* His hips flexed and he let go of her hands, cradling her head, pulling her down for another kiss.

The incoming tide whooshed against the bottoms of her feet. Water surged up her calves, cresting and releasing over and over until it swept around them completely.

She threw back her head as the stars melted and slid into the ocean. Then she collapsed onto Jeffrey's chest, body trembling as aftershocks of pleasure coursed through her body.

"You okay?" he asked, kissing her hair, stroking his hand down her back. His heavy breaths echoed in her ear.

"I'm fine," she breathed. "Completely, totally fine."

"You're a whole lot more than fine."

She could hear the smile in his voice.

He specified. "You are amazing. You are beyond amazing. You're my deepest, sweetest fantasy come to life."

Ashley pulled back a little to look him in the eyes. She grinned at the silly, absurd sentiment and shook her head in confusion. "Who are you and what have you done with Jeffrey Bradshaw?"

Jeffrey went silent for the space of several heartbeats. "It's complicated."

She gave a short chuckle. "Well that goes without saying."

"Really complicated."

Sure it was complicated. They were rivals, and they'd just made love. That was hardly simple. But it wasn't the end of the world either. They were both adults.

"Don't get so intense on me," she said. "Nothing has to change."

"Everything's changed."

"What is *with* you lately? Every time I turn around, you're doing something out of character."

"That's because I am."

"You are what?"

"Out of character."

"You're being obtuse."

He took a deep breath. "I just discovered I'm Jeffrey's long-lost twin brother from Alaska. The birthday—"

"*What?*" Had he *completely* lost his mind in New York? Developed a split personality?

"My name is Jordan Adamson."

"Is this a psychiatric thing?"

He shook his head. "It's the truth. We met by accident in the Alpine airport. Jeffrey's stuck in a blizzard up there, so I came down here to pitch his series."

He stared into her eyes, and she knew he was completely serious.

A sudden chill settled over her, as the horrible puzzle pieces fitted together.

He didn't talk like Jeffrey. He didn't act like Jeffrey. He'd been confused about the Platinum party. And the man ate *red meat.*

That wasn't Jeffrey. That was about as far from Jeffrey as you could get.

Reality threatened to suffocate her. She'd just made love to a stranger. A man who'd lied to her and deceived her.

She scrambled off him, and took a couple of steps down the beach, shock battling with anger battling with hurt.

How could Jeffrey...*Jordan* do this to her? Did the man have no conscience, no scruples, no honor?

Of course not.

He was Jeffrey's brother, through and through.

She straightened her spine.

Fine. If that's the way they wanted to play it.

She'd taken on one of them. She could take on the other.

If Jordan wanted to fight dirty, she'd show him how it was done in L.A. She turned to confront him, jabbing a finger in the air. "You want to take me on?"

Jordan pushed into a sitting position. "It's not—"

"Consider Jeffrey's promotion history."

"I—"

"When the Board finds out about this, he'll be lucky to keep his job."

"Ashley—"

"*No.* Don't you *dare* talk to me. Maybe this kind of behavior is acceptable in Alaska, but I find it despicable."

She rubbed the goose bumps on her arms. Did Jeffrey know Jordan had intended to seduce her? Was that part of the plan all along? Get past her defenses, then take her out?

"Did you really think you could woo me into giving up, and win by default?" she asked.

Jordan jumped to his feet. "What just happened between you and me had nothing to do with the job. Everything I ever said, everything I ever felt about you, is real.''

She scooped her damp sarong from the sand and knotted it around her waist. "Sure. And I should believe you because..."

"Because I'm telling the truth. I *told* you the truth. I didn't have to tell you who I was."

"Bad choice on your part then, wasn't it?"

His eyes narrowed. "Making love with you had *nothing* to do with the job."

"Everything's to do with the job. Haven't you figured that out yet? The job is all we do. It's who we are. It's—"

"This—" Jordan pointed his finger from her to him and back again "—was between you and me. Nobody else. Nothing else."

"Well, *I* was *me*. I just didn't realize *you* weren't *you*."

"*This* was about us."

Her voice rose in the night. "There is no us."

"Well, there sure as hell was three minutes ago."

Ashley stared at him in disgust, scooping her bikini top up from the ground and covering herself.

A look of concern crept into Jordan's expression, and he lowered his voice. "Jeffrey didn't set out to hurt you. He only sent me because he had absolutely no alternative. He had no idea that any of this—"

"There's *always* an alternative."

"You think he'd trust me with this if he could be here himself?"

"I really couldn't care less what Jeffrey would or would not do."

"If you'll just—"

"Forget it. I'm out of here." She dug her toes into the wet sand, turned and headed for the lights of the party.

JORDAN TOOK A STEP after her, then forced himself to stop, biting back her name instead of shouting it out loud. He clenched his fists and leaned back against the boulder that had sheltered them.

Could he have made it any worse? Was there any way in the world he could have more thoroughly screwed up everybody's life?

He grasped his sandy pants, only inches from the creeping waves, shaking them out and pulling them back on. The tie was lost somewhere in the dark, and he'd ruined his brother's jacket and shoes.

His brother.

Jordan leaned against the rock again.

He had a brother.

After thirty-four years of thinking he was completely alone in the world, there was someone else of the same lineage.

A band of imaginary steel tightened around his chest. What was he supposed to do with this?

He had to contact Jeffrey. But he couldn't do it while Jeffrey was in Katimuk.

This wasn't something he could do long distance. And it definitely wasn't something he could do over radio phone where half of Alaska could listen in.

He bent down and picked up the soggy shoes.

For now, he'd head back down the beach, back to the party, back to find Ashley before she could destroy Jeffrey's future.

Ashley.

Another band of steel trapped his chest, this one tighter than the last. He had to apologize to Ashley. He had to make her understand that he hadn't tried to hurt her.

And he had to change her mind about hurting Jeffrey.

5

ASHLEY LEFT the Platinum party without talking to another soul. She took a taxi to the office, then worked for two hours on her pilot series presentation before heading back to her apartment.

The series was improving. But she had to make it funnier. She had to make it shine.

She pressed the tenth floor button in the apartment elevator and watched the doors slide shut.

Even with Jeffrey out of the running, she needed to prove to the studio brass that she had *everything* it took to be a vice president. She needed to demonstrate her intelligence, her creativity, her hard work. She didn't want there to be any doubt in their minds that she'd be an asset to the company in the position.

Then they'd promote her with confidence.

And her future would be wonderful. She'd invite her father up to that top floor corner office. She'd give him her gold-embossed card, and he could brag to his friends about her the way he bragged about her brothers.

And she'd *love* her new job.

She'd love every single thing about it.

The elevator doors glided open, and she stepped out into her apartment hallway.

"Hi, Ashley."

She startled, jerking her chin up coming face-to-face with Jordan.

His jacket was gone, his shirt was damp and his hazel eyes were wary in the harsh hallway light.

"Go away," she rasped. She needed a hot bath, a hot drink and about a hundred hours of sleep.

"Did you do it?" he asked.

She elbowed past him and put her key into the lock. "Do what?"

"Cut Jeffrey off at the knees."

She turned to glare at Jordan.

She opened her mouth. Then closed it again.

She didn't owe him any explanations.

Truth was, she hadn't told anyone yet. She hadn't wanted to do it at the party and turn the story into a gossip fest. Not that Jeffrey didn't deserve it. Not that Jordan didn't deserve it.

"Can we talk?" asked Jordan.

She shook her head. "There's nothing left to say."

"There is if you haven't ruined his life yet."

She turned the knob on her apartment door. "You won't change my mind."

"Can I at least come in and try?"

"No."

"He's my *brother*." There was a pleading note in Jordan's voice that got to her.

She shook her head, not trusting herself to speak.

"Up until three hours ago I didn't have a family," he said. "Up until I saw his birthdate, I had no idea there was anyone on the planet related to me."

She recalled the expression of shock on Jordan's face. She'd toasted his birthday. Then he'd looked at his wallet, Jeffrey's wallet, Jeffrey's driver's license.

Jordan had left the party to cope with the revelation that he had a twin brother.

She'd lost her mother when she was only five. But she still had her father, and Aaron and Robert. She tried to imagine no family at all, and a wave of guilt crept into her system.

She squelched it.

She was sorry he'd been an orphan, but that didn't excuse his behavior. "You were wrong," she told him.

"I know."

"I don't owe you a thing."

"No, you don't."

"You won't change my mind."

"Maybe not."

She tipped her forehead against the door.

"Let me try?" he asked softly. "If you still disagree, I'll tell them myself tomorrow."

Ashley gave the door a firm shove with the flat of her hand, cursing herself for being a sap. There was something about that outer strength and inner vulnerability thing that got to her every time.

"Fine. You have five minutes. Get to it."

She marched into the apartment and grabbed a sweater from the hook in the front hallway, stuffing her arms in the sleeves.

Jordan followed her inside. "Right. Okay. Jeffrey's stranded in a blizzard in Alaska. No way to get out. No way to get home. I was his solution of last resort."

She kicked off her dirty sandals and headed for the living room. "And you think that makes it all right?"

Jordan stayed right behind her. "No. I think that explains his motivation. He wants that promotion as much as you do."

She crossed her arms over her chest and sank down into the overstuffed leather love seat beside her stone fireplace. "Enough to cheat for it?"

Jordan took the identical love seat opposite, staring at her across the glass table and her profusion of potted plants. "How is this cheating?"

She leaned forward. "Hello? You're pretending to be Jeffrey."

"And how is that cheating?"

Ashley shivered. She leaned over and flipped the switch on her gas fireplace. The flames leapt to life, orange flickers bouncing off her watercolor collection. "You're lying to everyone around you."

"But it doesn't help him. I could see if it was Jeffrey pretending to be me so that I could get a great studio job—"

Ashley rubbed her temples. "You're giving me a headache."

"My point is, sending me is not an advantage. In fact, it's a handicap."

"It's you winning the promotion, not Jeffrey."

Jordan shook his head. "Oh, no. It's Jeffrey's reputation, Jeffrey's work, Jeffrey's résumé. All I'm doing is delivering the presentation."

Ashley hesitated. Okay, she'd grant that having Jordan here was more of a disadvantage than a help. "That doesn't make it right."

"I'm not talking about right and wrong. I'm talking about necessity."

Ashley rubbed her arms. Even with the fire, she was cold. She needed Jordan to leave so that she could take a bath and have her hot drink. "And I'm talking about lying, deceit and deception."

Jordan paused. His green-brown eyes softened, and his shoulders drooped. "I'm sorry."

Ashley hopped up from her seat and crossed the room to the kitchen. Empathy was not an emotion that would keep her tough. She needed caffeine and she needed it now.

Jordan followed. "I was wrong. I was stupid. But you are *so* beautiful—"

"*Stop.*" Ashley had heard enough. It was bad enough that they'd made love, and she'd have to live with the mistake for the rest of her life, he didn't have to rehash the whole thing.

"I'm sorry," he repeated.

Ashley yanked open her freezer and pulled out the

coffee beans. She scooped them into the grinder, and pushed the button.

"Fine. Great," she shouted over the noise. "You're sorry it happened. I'm sorry it happened. We're both fools. But we can't go back. So can we please just forget about it?"

Jordan nodded. "Sure."

Ashley dumped the grounds into the coffeemaker and switched it on.

"I'll make you a deal," he said.

She shrugged. "Go ahead."

The hot coffee splattered and splashed into the carafe, filling the room with a deep, satisfying aroma.

She pulled up on tiptoe to reach for a coffee mug.

Jordan reached past her to help, and their fingertips met over the cup.

"Beat me fair and square," he said in a low, challenging voice, close to her ear.

She dropped back down on her heels, pulling the cup away from him, eyes narrowing. "Fair and square?"

"Let me compete. Let me try. I don't have much of a chance—"

"And let you both simply *get away with it?*"

"We're not getting away with anything. You've already agreed that I'm a handicap."

Ashley set the lone stoneware mug down on the counter, feeling churlish and rude. She reached for another. "Why should I give up a sure thing?"

"For your pride."

"I'd be a very proud vice president."

"But you'd never know for sure, would you?"

She turned to look into his eyes, understanding his point perfectly. But, he'd miscalculated. Her voice dropped. "I'd never care."

His mouth curved into a half smile. "Oh, yes, you would. You'd always wonder. You'd always know you took the coward's way—"

"Excuse me?"

"You know it's the truth. You're a fighter. If you thought you could win, you'd compete. The only reason you have to blow my cover is because you're afraid."

Ashley squared her shoulders. "I am not afraid of you. And I could beat you with one camera tied behind my back."

"Prove it."

"I don't need to."

"True enough. But we'll never know for sure unless you give me a shot." He cocked his head sideways.

She considered it. For a split second, she actually considered it.

But, that would be crazy. Jeffrey didn't deserve a chance, no matter how slim. And Jordan sure didn't deserve any breaks from her. They both deserved to be caught and face the consequences.

She pulled out the coffeepot and filled both the mugs.

"Come on, Ashley. Fair and square."

"And between now and Friday? What? We simply carry on, business as usual?"

"Why not?"

She picked up one of the mugs and shook her head, crossing back to the warm fireplace. "With no consequences for your deception? No comeuppance for Jeffrey?"

Jordan followed her and sat down again, taking a long drink of his coffee. "If you win, you'll know you earned it. If you rat me out, you'll have no proof that you really deserved the promotion."

She drank deeply, letting the caffeine hit her system and rev her up.

Jordan was wrong about that. She'd taken dozens of courses, spent endless nights working, toiled for years in the trenches in preparation for this chance. She'd battled her family's opinion, society's opinion. Her long climb up from the bottom of the heap had made her strong.

She *knew* she could win the promotion no matter who was up against her. Whether it be the real Jeffrey or the fake Jeffrey. She was confident in her talent, confident in her hard work.

"I have *earned* that promotion," she said.

"You can have it all, Ashley." He set his cup on the table. "The title, the money, the power... And Jeffrey's respect when he starts to work for you."

Ashley hesitated.

He had her on that one.

She could suddenly see the appeal of beating Jeffrey—even by proxy. Jeffrey might not be here in person, but he'd conceived the series Jordan was proposing. And Rob would do a good job putting together the presentation.

When she won, Jeffrey would have to admit she deserved it. He'd owe her his respect, and they'd both know it.

"Fine," she said with a decisive nod. "I'll give you two a shot. And I'll prove to both of you that I'm this company's first and best choice for vice president."

HE HAD A CHANCE.

At nine o'clock in the morning, Jordan closed his office door behind him and sighed into the big, empty room.

It wasn't a particularly good chance. But at least he wasn't completely out of the running.

He'd refocus on Jeffrey's pilot presentation and stay well away from Ashley. No matter how vivid the memories, no matter how much he wanted to make love with her again, he'd keep his distance.

She had her priorities and he had his. She'd be out of his life in a matter of days, and there was nothing he could do about that.

He had to think about his brother now.

And he was positive Jeffrey was his brother.

Just to be sure, he'd pulled Jeffrey's personnel files.

Jeffrey's birthplace was right there in black and white on the employee life insurance form. Jeffrey was also born in Seattle.

Jordan supposed they could do DNA tests at some point, but there wasn't a doubt in his mind that they were twins.

He stared at the telephone on the wide, mahogany desk, wondering if he should call his brother and give him an update.

It was a pretty daunting thought. There was no way to explain how he'd got caught without compromising Ashley. And he'd already decided to wait and break the news of their blood relationship in person.

Which left no reason to call. In fact, it left some damn good reasons not to call.

Besides, Jeffrey wouldn't be hanging around the Mush Lodge waiting for a radio call anyway. The weather reports said the storm was getting worse, and the residents of Katimuk would be holed up for the duration.

Jeffrey couldn't help him.

He'd have to get hold of Rob and—

The door to his office opened, and he turned around, expecting Bonnie.

Instead, Ashley marched in. Her hair was in another one of those tight French braids, showing off round, black and white swirl earrings. She was wearing a straight black skirt, a mannish white shirt and a black satin vest. Everything in her outfit and her posture said "don't mess with me."

She stared straight past him, not a single emotion on her face. "We have an assignment."

"We have?"

"Harold Gauthier wants us in the screening room at ten to review some pilot programs."

Oh, boy. Ashley and Jordan together. And Jordan expected to do studio work? "Review them for what?"

She met his eyes for a split second, shaking her head. "For midseason replacements. Focus group ratings are low on a couple of the new fall shows, and we need to have options ready for a midseason slot if the network drops something."

Oh, great. An assignment that mattered. This was not good. "I don't think that's such a great idea."

"Oh, really?" she scoffed. "You don't?"

"How do I get out of it?"

"Don't you think I *tried* to get you out of it? Hanging around the screening room for hours on end doing both mine and Jeffrey's work is not my idea of a good time."

"I'm stuck?"

"No, actually, I'm stuck. You're just along for the ride."

Jordan cringed. "Right. Sorry."

"So you've said." She turned to leave.

"Ashley?"

She paused with her hand on the door.

"What?"

"Where's the screening room?"

"Eighteenth floor, end of the west hallway."

"Thanks."

With a sharp nod, she opened the door and exited the office.

So much for staying away from her for the next couple of days. Plan B would have to be squelching his libido and staying out of range.

WHEN JORDAN ARRIVED at the screening room, he expected to find Ashley there alone. To his surprise, there was another man standing talking to her.

Jordan frowned.

The man was standing way too close. And she didn't want him that close. Easiest thing in the world to see given her body language.

Her whole upper body was tipped back. Her jaw was set and her blue eyes were icy with suspicion.

Jordan headed across the opulent room to join them.

It was windowless. The walls were papered in a deep green, and there were rich burgundy easy chairs set up on several descending levels, facing a big screen at the far end of the room. The small tables between the chairs were marble-topped, their legs ornately carved cherry wood.

This was definitely where the rich and famous came to watch television.

"Ashley," Jordan nodded, walking up to the pair and eyeing the strange man.

"Hey, Jeff, my man," the stranger said, clapping Jordan on the shoulder and reaching out to shake. "Great to see you back," he said a little too heartily, and Jordan sensed the man didn't like his brother.

They were rivals of some kind. But why?

He glanced over at Ashley, hoping against hope she'd bail him out.

"Carl came over from Metro Productions to watch the pilots with us," she said, without looking at Jordan.

Jordan tried to catch her eye. He wanted to convey his thanks for providing the man's name. But she refused to focus above his chest level.

He turned his attention back to Carl. "How've you been, Carl?"

"Couldn't be better," said Carl. "The ratings are high, my debts are low and my ex-wife moved to Sacramento." He winked at Jordan with a buddy, buddy, long-suffering, women-are-a-ball-and-chain grin.

Offended on both Ashley and the ex-wife's behalf, Jordan's opinion of the man plummeted. Not that it had started off very high in the first place.

He wasn't crazy about large, gold earrings and the unshaven look. And he'd always hated men who winked. It was as if they had to explain a joke that hadn't quite come off.

"We might as well get started on the Q-23s" said Ashley, heading for one of the side tables. Her lips were pursed, and her shoulders looked tense.

Jordan wished he could ask her what was wrong.

"I've queued up *Anchors Aweigh* to start," she said, returning with three leather-bound clipboards and gold pens. She handed one to each of the men.

Jordan stared at his in confusion. Since he could hardly ask questions about Q-23s, he hoped he could sit behind her and cheat over her shoulder.

"Anybody else want a drink?" asked Carl, ambling over to what was obviously a bar.

He wore loose white trousers, a gauzy shirt and string sandals. The square-link gold chain around his neck matched the ostentatious earring.

When Jordan and Ashley didn't answer, Carl turned and held up a bottle of scotch.

"Nothing for me," said Jordan. It was barely ten o'clock in the morning.

"No thanks," said Ashley, sitting down at the end of one row and picking up a remote control.

Carl turned back to the bar and began scooping ice from the silver bucket.

Jordan leaned down to Ashley. "Who is that guy?" he whispered.

She finally looked him in the eyes. "Our competition," she murmured.

"Our *what?*"

"Nothing like twelve-year-old single malt," said Carl. His gaze flitted shrewdly from Ashley to Jordan and back again. "What are you two whispering about?"

Jordan slowly straightened. "Your earring."

Carl reached up to finger the bauble. "Got it in Madrid," he said.

"Nice," said Jordan, not quite able to keep the sarcasm from his voice.

He determinedly took the seat next to Ashley. He knew having him that close would annoy her, but he didn't want Carl sitting there.

To his irritation, Carl took the seat directly behind her. Now he was the one who could look over her shoulder.

"*Anchors Aweigh,*" said Ashley, crossing her legs, her gaze fixed firmly on the screen. She hit one button to dim the overhead lights, and another to start the tape.

Her foot twitched rhythmically in the air and she clicked and unclicked the pen above her clipboard.

What had she meant that Carl was their competition? Their competition in what? Would they have to fight over which pilot to choose? As far as Jordan was concerned, the two of them could pick any pilot they wanted. He didn't have the slightest idea.

Anchors Aweigh was about a single mother who inherited a broken-down fishing resort and brought her punk rock, rebellious daughter to live amongst a group of crotchety senior citizens. It was fast-paced and zany. A bit overly zany for Jordan's taste.

About halfway through the show, one of the older men seemed to develop a leering crush on the single mother. Though the canned laughter made light of the issue, Jordan thought it was crass and offensive.

He heard Carl chuckle behind him, and he glanced over at Ashley to try to gauge her reaction.

Her eyes were wide, and she was pressed back in her chair.

"Do you think it's supposed to be funny?" Jordan whispered.

Ashley shrugged her shoulders without looking at him.

The older man put out a hand to help the single mother into a small rowboat. He patted her butt as she stepped off the dock, and the camera zoomed in on his leer.

Jordan wanted to slug him.

Carl whistled low. "Look out, mama."

Jordan bit back a rude retort.

The episode ended with the rebellious teenager showing off her pierced navel to one of the senior citizens.

Ashley hit the remote control button, and the screen went black. She and Carl immediately began scribbling notes on their Q-23 forms.

Jordan opened his clipboard and stared at the categories. He hadn't the first clue what to write.

He leaned slightly sideways, hoping to catch a glimpse of Ashley's notes, but it was too dark, and her writing was too messy from this distance.

He decided to take the entire problem to Rob later. He pretended to write until the other two stopped, then he quickly closed his book on the blank pages.

"Next one's an untitled reality TV series. Set in northern Canada." Ashley's voice was painfully impersonal, and her movements crisp as she reached for the remote control once more. She hadn't once looked Jordan's way since they sat down.

He told himself it was better this way. If they stayed cool, professional and detached, they couldn't get themselves into any more trouble. He needed to focus on Jeffrey not Ashley.

Not that Ashley was about to let him focus on her.

Still, he couldn't help a sidelong glance at her profile. Even when she was playing the iron maiden, she was incredibly beautiful. And she was obviously intelligent. And, when she relaxed, she had a great sense of humor.

A parka-clad man had appeared on screen, standing in front of what looked like a plastic igloo. He proceeded to explain the rules of a bizarre survival game. The fact that you couldn't even see the man's breath in the "harsh northern conditions," really undermined the credibility of the whole setup.

Contestants were paired off into couples, and the couples were grouped into villages. As near as he could tell, the object of the "game" was to build an igloo, run a dog team and survive on raw fish for two weeks.

There also seemed to be some romantic matchmaking element involved. Though the couples switched partners with the regularity of a square dance. And some creative genius had written in a convenient hot spring, which seemed to come complete with naturally occurring champagne.

But, what really killed it for him was the firewood. Where the hell did they get firewood out on the pack ice?

"I'd just cook the freakin' fish," he finally muttered.

"They're not allowed to," said Carl.

"Where did that hot spring come from?" Jordan pressed, offended on behalf of northerners. "Did it just bubble up from beneath the Beaufort Sea?"

"Artistic license," said Ashley.

"It's ridiculous," said Jordan.

"Who cares?" asked Carl. "With babes like those, it's gonna sell like hotcakes."

"You think people are going to buy that cedar firewood grows on icebergs?"

"Never overestimate the intelligence of the viewing public," said Carl. "What the hell happened to you in New York?"

Jordan didn't answer.

Ashley hit the remote control and scribbled some more notes on her form.

Jordan scrawled *it sucks* across his. Not that he was likely to forget that information when he talked to Rob.

Carl stood up from his chair and made a big show of stretching. "Gotta go to the can."

"Thank you for sharing that," muttered Jordan.

Ashley shot him a look that he couldn't interpret.

"Don't do anything I wouldn't do," said Carl as he sauntered toward the door.

As soon as it swung shut behind him, Jordan turned to Ashley. "Who the hell is that guy?"

She stopped writing and finally met his eyes. "Our competition."

"What does that *mean?*"

"He wants the job?"

"*Our* job?"

Her eyes went dull. "Yeah."

Jordan paused. "Does he have a good chance?"

Her gaze swung to the closed door, then she nodded. "Yeah."

Jordan swore.

6

ASHLEY PICKED UP the jade paperweight from her desk and clenched it in her fist. She wished she was the kind of person to throw it at something. She wished she could hurl it toward the mirror on her office wall and watch the glass shatter to the floor like her life.

She'd lost the vice president's job.

When she'd walked into the screening room to see Carl Nedesco standing there, straight out of left field, a smug expression on his face, she'd been stunned.

She'd known immediately what it meant. One, the pilot evaluations were part of the test. And two, Carl had also been shortlisted for the vice president's job.

And here she'd thought Jeffrey was the problem.

The door to her office opened. "Ashley?"

Jordan's voice. Identical to Jeffrey's voice.

"I want to talk," he stated.

She turned to face him. "There's nothing to talk about. Not anymore. Carl's going to beat us both."

She wasn't stupid, and she wasn't suicidal. Carl was powerful and vindictive. There was a time to fight the good fight, and a time to conserve your strength.

Jordan clicked the door shut behind him, heading into the room.

"What makes you so sure?" he asked.

Ashley didn't answer. She turned away, plunking the paperweight back down on the desk, gazing out her picture window at the cars snaking along the expressway, trying not to let depression overwhelm her.

"My dad was wrong," she said. "He always warned me there was a glass ceiling. He told me to back off, not to set my aspirations so high. He worried that I'd get hurt trying to break through."

She turned to look at Jordan again. "But it's not a glass ceiling. It's a box. A glass box where women like me get stuck.

"We can't see it. We can't feel it. We can't break it. But it's always there, holding us in, never letting us stretch."

Jordan's brows knitted together.

"You have no idea what I'm talking about, do you?"

"I'm guessing it has something to do with Carl and the promotion."

Ashley laughed darkly. "I can't beat him. It's not because he's smarter. It's not because he has more experience. It's not because he's better for the company..."

Maybe she should quit. Just quit Argonaut now and get it over with. She couldn't work for Carl. She couldn't walk into this office day after day and try to do her job with that man calling the shots.

Maybe her father had been right all along. She

should have taken the safe road, limited her risks. Disappointment overwhelmed her.

Jordan moved in a little closer. "I don't get it. You thought you could beat Jeffrey. What's the difference?"

"Jeffrey's been away. He's been in New York for a year. And even if he wasn't, he doesn't have the connections Carl has. Jeffrey's a man, but he's a bit of an outsider. I've been on the inside for a while now, and that balances us out."

"But Carl's got both," said Jordan in an understanding voice.

She nodded, pressing her fingertips against her forehead. "Carl's got both."

Jordan moved up beside her, his shoulder brushing lightly against hers. He lifted the round, green paperweight and tested it in his palm. He tossed it lightly in the air and caught it again, holding it up to the light.

"Could Jeffrey beat Carl?" he asked.

Ashley shrugged. "Maybe. If he was here. Toe-to-toe, he could probably give Carl a run for his money."

"Would that be better? Would you rather have Jeffrey as vice president?"

Ashley grimaced. "The devil himself would be better than Carl Nedesco."

Jordan set the paperweight back down. "How about me?"

"You what?"

He looked her straight in the eye. "Me as Jeffrey."

Ashley's eyebrows crept up. "You mean take on Carl?"

Jordan gave her a calculating smile. "Yeah. I think I'd like that."

Not a chance. Carl would eat Jordan for lunch.

Ashley shook her head. "He's got a lock on half the Board members starting out. And you...no offense, but you're clueless."

"You could help me."

"Help you get the job?"

"Help Jeffrey get the job?"

She laughed. She couldn't help it. Her help Jeffrey Bradshaw? The very idea was preposterous.

"I fooled you," said Jordan in a low voice.

Ashley felt a shift in the atmosphere, and her gaze was drawn to him. "Not completely."

His eyes darkened. He reached for her hand, encircling her fingers, stroking the pad of his thumb over her knuckles. "Yeah, but they'll never get anywhere *near* what it was that gave me away with you."

A pulse of awareness leapt through Ashley, and she quickly withdrew her hand. "Exactly what are you proposing? That I lip-synch you through the interview?"

"So far, they haven't scheduled an interview."

"They didn't schedule the pilot evaluations, either, but, trust me, they're part of the test."

"You can help me with the Q-23s, and help me

make the pilot project even better. And Jeffrey's résumé seems pretty solid."

Ashley shook her head. This was the craziest idea she'd ever heard. "It's nowhere near that simple."

Jordan stood up straight. He drew back his shoulders. He tilted his head, squinted his eyes and lifted his chin up just so.

His voice took on a hard, demanding edge. "What do you mean, I'm not getting a promotion? I *flew* here for a promotion. I *deserve* a promotion. I *demand* my promotion."

He was Jeffrey. Good grief he was Jeffrey all over. Ashley blinked in amazement. "Wow."

Jordan relaxed and gave a self-deprecating shrug. "I guess I wasn't really trying all that hard before."

"How did you *do* that?"

"I clench up real tight and pretend I own the world."

Ashley had to fight a brief grin. "You do it very well."

"Thank you. So, you want to help me beat Carl?"

Oh, boy. Ashley squeezed her eyes shut, silently railing that fate had done this to her.

It was bad enough she'd already lost. But now she had to choose. She could either sit back and watch Carl take over the entire acquisitions department, or help Jeffrey Bradshaw achieve *her* dream.

Jeffrey or Carl.

The only thing she knew for sure was that Carl was unacceptable.

JORDAN COULD almost see Ashley's spine stiffening. Her eyes opened and her chin tipped up.

"We're going to need something with Jeffrey's handwriting," she said. "And I'm going to need to see your whole pilot project. Right now."

Jordan felt a wave of optimism rise within him. Maybe all wasn't lost. He couldn't do anything about Carl's advantage over Ashley. But, together, they might be able to help each other. "Is that a yes?"

Ashley picked up her phone and punched in a number. "It's not a *yes* to Jeffrey. It's a *no* to Carl. Make no mistake about it, you and Jeffrey have simply moved to number two on my hit list."

Quite frankly, Jordan was grateful to be number two on Ashley's hit list.

"Rachel? It's Ashley. Can you meet me in the lobby in half an hour?"

Her gaze slid to Jordan as she listened for a moment. "Yeah. It's about the promotion."

Another pause. "Great. See you then."

She disconnected the line and held the receiver out to Jordan. "Call Rob. Get him to meet us downstairs as soon as he can. We've got exactly forty-eight hours to do the impossible."

Jordan accepted the telephone receiver. "Anybody ever tell you you've got a lot of class?"

She glanced away, seemingly embarrassed.

Jordan punched in Rob's cell phone number.

"Rob here."

"Rob. It's Jordan. Ashley and I need your help."

Rob's voice was immediately suspicious. "Ashley?"

"Yeah. Ashley. She knows about me."

"Knows what?"

"She knows I'm Jordan. She's right here. She wants to help—"

"It's a trick," said Rob.

"It's not a trick," said Jordan.

Ashley scooped the phone from his hand. "Rob?" She sighed. "No."

Her eyes narrowed. "Of *course* not.

"Carl Nedesco is on the shortlist, that's what.

"Yeah. I know.

"Right. See you then."

She grabbed her leather clipboard from the top of the desk, and headed for the office door. "Let's go get that writing sample. And I sure hope you're a decent forger."

ASHLEY STOOD on the beach next to Rachel while Rob and the crew set up for a kayak action sequence. They'd found a spot on shore where a rugged rock channel and a powerful tidal rush would pass as a river. And they were filming toward the ocean so the vegetation wouldn't give them away.

It wasn't perfect as an Alaskan setting, but Rob and

Ashley had both agreed the kayak film clip would make a great addition to the pilot presentation. And when Jordan had offered to act as stuntman, they'd thrown everything together within an hour.

Rachel shaded her eyes and stared at Jordan where he stood beside the kayak, paddle in hand. "So, you're saying, all evidence to the contrary, that's *not* Jeffrey Bradshaw."

"Right," said Ashley.

"Unbelievable," said Rachel.

Ashley squinted across the hot sand. "It took me a while, but it's fairly easy to tell them apart, once you see—"

Jordan's voice carried across the sand as he spoke to Rob. "*Nobody* goes kayaking in Alaska without a shirt."

"Theatric license," said Rob.

"Mosquito bait," said Jordan, but he stripped off his T-shirt and stood there in nothing but a pair of trunks.

Ashley caught her breath.

"The women of the western world want to ogle your pecs," said Rob.

Ashley wasn't about to argue with that one. Jordan's pecs were a sight to behold. Too bad the entire board of directors for Argonaut were men.

Rachel elbowed Ashley in the arm to get her attention. "Once you see *what?*"

"Think we got what we needed on that last tracking shot?" asked Ashley, trying not to remember the event that had tipped her off to Jordan's identity—at least not in too much detail.

Rachel crossed her arms over her chest. "Uh-uh. No dice. You're not getting away that easily."

"Because if we didn't get it right," Ashley continued, "I guess we'll fix it up in cutting."

Rachel leaned forward. "Ashley. Finish your sentence."

Ashley turned to look at her friend, trying to keep her expression from revealing too much.

But, given the way Rachel's eyes sparkled, she didn't think she was successful.

"I did finish my sentence," said Ashley, unable to resist teasing Rachel a bit longer. Of course she was going to crack and tell her. She always did.

"You said they're easy to tell apart once you *see*," said Rachel. "That means he did something or said something…"

Ashley brushed her hair off her face, turning her attention back to Jordan, zeroing in on his bare shoulders. "Once you see that there are two of them."

Rachel shook her head. "Uh-uh. That's not it. Something happened between you two. What was it?"

"Okay. Here's the truth. He said, 'My name's Jordan Adamson. I'm Jeffrey's long-lost twin brother from Alaska.'"

Rachel's face fell. "Oh. I guess that would do it."

Ashley watched Jordan and Rob wade out into the

surf. Rob held the kayak steady while Jordan climbed in and settled the rubber skirt around his hips.

"It was right after I asked him who he was, and what he'd done with Jeffrey." Ashley paused. "That was right after we made wild and passionate love on the beach."

Rachel jerked her head around to stare at Ashley. "You *what?*"

Jordan paddled backward, away from Rob, his shoulders and arms flexing with each stroke.

Ashley's mouth went dry, as her memories crowded in. She remembered the feel of his muscles, the taste of his skin. Whatever else had happened between them, there was no denying that making love with Jordan had been one of the most sensuous and erotic experiences of her life.

Rachel grabbed her arm. "Ashley, you made love with Jeffrey Bradshaw?"

"No. I made love with Jordan Adamson."

"But you didn't know it was Jordan at the time."

Ashley paused. "Not at first. Not for sure."

"But you figured it out, when? Like partway?"

"Sort of."

"Oh, *my*, *God*."

"Keep your voice down."

Rachel leaned a little closer. "Inquiring minds *have* to know. *What* gave him away."

"Everything. Nothing. All kinds of little things. Plain and simple, he's just not Jeffrey."

"Details. I want details."

Ashley smiled to herself. "Forget it."

Rob called to the crew as he paced out of the water. "Remember this is supposed to be a river. I want lots of close-up action on Jordan, and some selective focus. Get the whitewater but not the waves. Barry? Can you move up on the outcropping? Watch out for the shadows from the hills."

Ashley stared at Jordan, bobbing out there in the surf. He looked like a Greek god—water shimmering off his bare skin, dark hair slicked back, muscles straining against the kayak paddle as he made his way around huge, half-submerged boulders.

"You can't leave me hanging like this," said Rachel.

"It happened. It's over. He'll be gone in two days."

Rachel blinked. "That's it?"

Ashley cleared her throat. "That's it."

That was pretty much all there was to their torrid relationship. She had to forget about it now, because there was nowhere they could go from here.

"But if it was wild and passionate…"

"When I found out he was Jordan, I was pretty upset," she confessed. "It didn't exactly end on good terms. I said some things… He said some things…"

"But you're helping him now."

"Only to thwart Carl."

"Can't say I blame you on that one," said Rachel, shifting her gaze back to Rob and the crew. "Carl's a pig."

"Can you *imagine* what'll happen to the studio if he takes over?"

"Tabloid television," said Rachel. "The ratings would probably skyrocket."

Ashley shook her head. Carl would keep the Board and the shareholders happy while demoralizing the staff.

"Wait for a big one," Rob shouted to Jordan. "Then come in through the cut."

He gestured to an opening between two big rocks. "Can you turn sideways halfway through and then do a roll?"

Jordan nodded.

"He's going to *roll over?*" asked Rachel.

"I guess so." Ashley felt a knot of tension form in her stomach. Was it safe? Did Jordan know how to do that sort of thing?

"I think we've got a big one coming," Rob called. "Rolling..." He motioned with his hand to the camera crew.

Jordan paddled furiously as a big wave came up from behind. He headed for the passage between the rocks. The surge of water foamed against them. He disappeared behind a rock for a moment, then shot back into sight, careening at an angle, turning sideways and flipping upside down.

The bow of the kayak pivoted sharply and banged into one of the rocks.

Ashley held her breath. A second went by, then three, then five. Her fingers dug into her palms.

"Rob?" she asked.

Rob took a couple of steps into the water.

Suddenly Jordan turned upright, shaking his head and digging in with his paddle. She could see blood well up from a scrape on his shoulder.

"Did you get it?" Rob asked the camera operators.

There were nods all around.

"Hot damn," Rob shouted. "You okay, Jord?"

"Hell of an undertow," Jordan called, raking his wet hair back with his fingers, breathing deeply. "You need me to do it again?"

"Can you?" asked Rob.

"Uh, Rob..." Ashley stepped forward about to protest.

But Jordan nodded his agreement before she could speak. He started the long paddle around the boulders to get in position again.

"Let me get this straight," said Rachel. "It was great sex."

"Yeah."

"With him."

Ashley swallowed. "Yeah."

"Then you fought."

"Right."

"And now you're keeping your distance because he lied to you and he's leaving in two days."

Ashley could feel her hard-won resolve starting to crumble. "Uh-huh."

Rachel sighed. "You made the right decision. But the right decision's a bitch sometimes, isn't it?"

"FINISHED MY ASSIGNMENT, teacher," Jordan announced, as he shut the door to Ashley's office behind him. It was nearly ten o'clock at night. They'd filmed for the rest of the afternoon. Then while Ashley and Rob worked with the film clips, Jordan had transcribed Ashley's Q-23 forms into Jeffrey's handwriting.

It had been amazingly easy to forge Jeffrey's handwriting. He guessed there was something about twins that influenced their fine motor skills.

As he read through Ashley's analysis of the shows, he was very impressed. She'd predicted the effect of elements that Jordan hadn't even noticed.

She rose from her chair and walked around the desk to meet him, holding out her hand for the paper. "Let me see?"

"Where's Rob?"

"He just left." She looked from Jordan's notes to Jeffrey's writing sample and back again. "Pretty good."

Jordan shrugged. "Luck of genetics."

She blinked her obviously tired eyes and gave her head a little shake. "I'm about done. Rob's going to meet us to work on the storyboard at eight tomorrow morning. You might as well go home and get some sleep."

Jordan was encouraged by her relaxed, conversational tone. Maybe she was getting over her anger.

"What are you doing for dinner?" he asked.

Her shoulders stiffened, and those don't-mess-with-me signals started up again. She backed away from him. "Eating."

Jordan sighed. Underneath the tough veneer, Ashley was a wonderful woman, and she was doing a great thing for Jeffrey under really difficult circumstances. He hated the tension between them.

He tried again. "I thought we could get something together. Maybe talk a bit. Maybe…"

She moved around behind her desk, putting it between them like a barrier. "I don't think that's a good idea."

"Why not? We're on the same team now."

She busied herself with some papers on her desktop, purposely not looking at him. "We're *not* on the same team. I made a deal with the devil—"

"The *devil?*"

"Yes.

"Isn't that a bit of an exaggeration?" Sure, he'd deceived her, but it was for a good cause. And he didn't think it made him evil incarnate.

Her mouth pursed tight, and she still didn't look up. "Not in my opinion."

He knew he should leave it at that. But he just

couldn't bring himself to give up. She was the most fascinating woman he'd ever come across, and there was some kind of inexplicable, electric current that seemed to hover in the air between them.

He wanted to know what it was. And he wanted to convince her he wasn't such a bad guy. In less than two days, he'd be gone. Who knew if he'd ever see her again? It was suddenly very important to him that they part without her hating him.

"Just give me a chance," he pressed. "I promise I won't pull anything overtly evil during the entrée."

She opened a drawer and rattled through some pens and paper clips.

He took a step closer. "Can I be perfectly honest?"

She didn't look up. "That would be refreshing."

"I like you, Ashley." The words came out huskier than he'd intended. He cleared his throat. "You're doing me a big favor, and I really don't want us to leave it like this."

"I'm not doing it for you," she said. Then she straightened, looking in his general direction. Not quite *at* him, but it was an improvement. "And we're fine. You can go now."

"Let me take you out. Somewhere nice. To thank you on Jeffrey's behalf. Maybe I can spend a couple of hours as Jordan Adamson, tourist from Alaska instead of studio executive imposter. It's the first time I've been to California."

She shook her head. "Sorry. No can do."

Leave, he told himself. *Before you make her mad again. For Jeffrey's sake, take what she's willing to give and quit messing around.*

"Why not?" he asked, ignoring common sense.

"I've got..." She glanced somewhat frantically around the office.

"You've got what?" he prompted.

"Grocery shopping."

"*Grocery* shopping?"

"Yeah," she nodded, obviously lying through her teeth. "With all the work getting the presentation ready this week, I haven't had time for anything else. Groceries, laundry, shower. I've got a packed night ahead of me." She started moving toward the office door.

"You've got to eat sometime," he said, calling her bluff.

"I'll toss something in the microwave when I get back from the store." She brushed past him.

"I'll help," he offered, as she put her hand on the doorknob.

He took a quick step to catch up with her. "I'll help you grocery shop, then we can throw something together while your laundry dries." He didn't mention the shower, though his pulse thrummed at the image.

Even so, he'd behave himself, he promised. If she agreed to spend some time with him, he'd do his very best to repair their relationship and forget about *anything* sexual.

He held her gaze with his own. "What do you say?"

She bit her bottom lip. "I don't think—"

"It'll be great. I bet L.A. grocery stores are much more exciting than the co-op in Alpine."

Her eyebrows crept up. "Exciting?"

"In Alpine we have five thousand people and one store. We get lettuce once a week, milk on Tuesdays and Fridays."

"You're kidding."

"You have no idea how thrilling I'll find your produce section." He turned and opened the office door, gesturing for her to precede him. "Not to mention the international cheeses. I've got Jeffrey's car downstairs."

THIS WAS A BAD IDEA. Ashley could not *begin* to enumerate the ways in which this was a bad idea.

The worst part was that she didn't even need groceries. Okay, that wasn't the worst part. The worst part was that Jordan—grocery-deprived, Alaskan hard-body—seemed determined to stick to her like glue.

She grabbed a cart from the row outside the entrance.

"Let me." Jordan reached for the handle, and she pulled her hands out of the way. Last thing in the world she needed was to touch him.

Watching his gleaming wet body this afternoon had

been enough of a torture. Touching him might just kill her.

"Which way?" he asked as they wheeled through the automatic doors and under the fluorescent lights.

"You tell me. You're the one on the adventure."

Carts clattered, cash registers beeped and seventies rock music streamed from cheap overhead speakers. He'd said he wanted to play tourist. As tourist highlights in California went, this was hardly on the A-list.

"What do you need?" he asked, glancing around at the long aisles that stretched to the back of the megastore.

"Fruit," she said, figuring she could always use a few extra vitamins.

"Fruit it is." He wheeled the cart ninety degrees and headed off toward the produce section. There the lighting was softer, green tinged beneath the low false ceiling.

Ashley trailed behind, deciding it was safer if they weren't talking. That was, until she realized she was watching his butt—fixating on his butt, to be more precise.

She quickened her pace until she was walking beside him again. At least here she could look straight ahead and keep him out of her vision.

"Apples?" he asked. "Oranges? Bananas?"

Too bad she could still hear that sexy voice. And too bad she could smell his spicy aftershave.

"Holy cow," he quickened his pace. "We have *got* to get some of these."

"What?"

"Kiwis. Only thirty cents apiece."

"You want to spend *thirty cents* on a kiwi?"

"Have you ever tried one?" He picked up two of the small, brown, fuzzy fruits, held them under his nose and inhaled.

"Of course I've tried them."

"These are huge." He cradled them in his palm, gazing with near reverence.

"You really are deprived, aren't you?"

"And look at that." He was off again.

Ashley trotted to keep up.

"Peaches. You need some peaches?" A kid in a candy store had nothing on him.

"Uh, sure," she answered.

"We can't get them like this in Alaska. Not at any price. It's almost worth carrying some home in my lap."

Ashley shook her head. She knew she shouldn't be feeling all mushy and compassionate, but his produce innocence was kind of sweet.

A wayward part of her brain wanted to take him home, kiss his brow and feed him peach slices.

Okay, so she wanted to kiss other parts of his body, too. And she was naked in the peach-feeding vision.

So was he.

She plucked at the neckline of her T-shirt, whooshing the cool, air-conditioned air over her breasts. She was so weak-willed. Who would have thought grocery shopping could do her in.

"Jordan?" The question was out before she could stop it.

"Yeah?"

Don't make it worse, the nonwayward part of her brain warned. "We could make a fruit salad back at my place."

"Yeah? That'd be great." He grinned and her heart flip-flopped.

Brilliant move. Positively brilliant. Just take the nice devil home.

"Can we get grapes?" he asked.

"Whatever."

He reached forward to brush a wisp of hair from her cheek. "You're a peach."

Ashley groaned, even as the force of his light touch overtook her nervous system.

"Sorry." He didn't look the least bit sorry. "Couldn't resist."

"You really have to get out more often." And she really had to get her legs to stop buzzing. At this rate, she was going to melt into a puddle on the floor before they made it past the bakery.

"I have to admit, I think that myself every May while I'm waiting for the ice to break up."

"You have ice in May?"

He nodded. "You like melons?" He lifted a honey-dew and rapped his knuckles on the rind.

"Like this." She reached for the round, light green melon. Her fingertips brushed his, and she froze for a split second.

"You, uh, go by weight." She forced herself to move away from his touch, hoisting the fruit in both hands. "And smell." She lifted it under her nose. "When they're sweet, they're ripe."

"Good one?" he asked.

She nodded. "Great one."

"You find me some strawberries to go with it, and I'm yours for life."

By life, he only meant thirty-six hours, she reminded herself. "You're going back to Alpine day after tomorrow."

He removed the melon from her hands and took a sniff. "Ah, yes. Back to Alpine. Where there's two feet of snow and no honeydews."

"Is that where Jeffrey's stuck?" She forced herself to concentrate on something other than Jordan's sex appeal.

"Jeffrey's stuck in Katimuk."

"Where's Katimuk?" She started for the bakery section. A loaf of French bread and some brie cheese would offset the fruit salad—nothing sexy about bread and cheese.

"A few hundred miles north of Alpine. It's pretty remote up there." He wheeled along beside her.

"Remote compared to a town with one grocery store and dairy deliveries only twice a week?"

"Oh, yeah. Jeffrey's eating homemade French fries and moose steak at the Mush Lodge. He's going to be in the mood for peaches by the time he gets back."

"The Mush Lodge?"

"Only business establishment there is in Katimuk."

Despite everything, Ashley couldn't help but grin. "I would pay serious money to see that." She picked up a loaf of bread, holding it in the air and questioning Jordan with her eyes.

Jordan nodded a yes, and she put it in the cart.

Then she picked up a package of brie from the deli cooler.

"What's that?"

"Cheese. You must have tried brie."

He shook his head. "But I'm game. Can we get some steaks or something to go with this?"

"What about a nice boneless chicken breast?"

"I need cholesterol."

"You might look like Jeffrey, but you sure don't act like him."

Jordan's voice dropped, and he leaned into her shoulder as they walked. "Is that a good thing or a bad thing?"

"Depends." Uh-oh. There went her knees again. Jordan was a good thing—a very good thing. He was also a very bad thing.

"On what?" he asked, maintaining contact with her shoulder.

A bad thing, because she wanted him. Even though he'd lied, and even though he was leaving, she still wanted him with an intensity that eclipsed reason.

That was why he was bad.

It was also why he was good.

"Do you like it in Alaska?" she asked, taking the coward's way out.

"Huh?" He pulled back from her shoulder and swung around to look at her.

"Alaska. Between the cold, the snow and the shocking lack of groceries, it doesn't seem like a very nice place."

"I love it in Alaska. It's peaceful, quiet. And the people are friendly and supportive. We don't compete the way you Californians do."

"Are you insinuating that Alaskans are better people than Californians?"

"No," he chuckled, snagging a package of T-bones as they passed the meat display. "I don't insinuate."

"I'm not eating that," she said.

"It's full of iron."

"Heart attack on a plate."

He shook his head as he tossed it into the cart. "What I'm saying is we have to be nice to each other. There's no anonymity in a town of five thousand people. Cut somebody off in traffic, and you might end up

Play The Lucky Hearts Game

and get...
FREE BOOKS & a FREE GIFT...
YOURS to KEEP!

Yes! I have scratched off the silver card. Please send me my **FREE BOOKS** and **FREE MYSTERY GIFT**. I understand that I am under no obligation to purchase any books as explained on the back of this card. I am over 18 years of age.

Scratch Here! then look below to see what you can claim...

T4CI

Mrs/Miss/Ms/Mr _____ Initials _____

BLOCK CAPITALS PLEASE

Surname _____

Address _____

_____

Postcode _____

Twenty-one gets you
2 FREE BOOKS and a
MYSTERY GIFT!

Twenty gets you
1 FREE BOOK and a
MYSTERY GIFT!

Nineteen gets you
1 FREE BOOK!

TRY AGAIN!

NO STAMP
NEEDED!

THE READER SERVICE™
FREE BOOK OFFER
FREEPOST CN81
CROYDON
CR9 3WZ

NO STAMP
NECESSARY
IF POSTED IN
THE U.K. OR N.I.

in their grocery lineup a week later. Worse, you might end up as a guest at their wedding."

Ashley picked up a package of boneless, skinless chicken breasts. "Everybody knows everybody else's business?"

"I'm not eating that," he said.

"It's full of low-fat protein." She stuck it in the cart.

"Sometimes they know your business," he said, as they cut through the frozen foods section toward the checkouts. "On the other hand, it's pretty easy to find privacy if that's what you want. My house is on ten acres, right on the shore of Glacier Lake. You can walk for miles out back and never see another soul."

"Jeffrey must be flipping out." If Jordan was describing Alpine, Katimuk was beyond the back of beyond.

"Given the tone of my few radio communications with him—yeah, I'd say flipping out was a good way to put it."

Ashley smiled. "Incredibly, there's a silver lining in all this after all."

They came to a halt at the end of a long checkout lineup, and Jordan's expression turned serious. "Only one silver lining?"

Desire thudded insistently through her body. Her chest tightened, her limbs tingled and her fingertips itched to touch him.

Did she want to flirt with him? If she wanted to play with fire, he'd handed her a perfect opening.

"Maybe two," she didn't quite commit herself.

He leaned toward her so that none of the other patrons would overhear. "I have to ask—"

"You ever get lonely up there?" she rushed in.

"You ever stay on topic?"

She felt her cheeks heat.

"Okay. Sorry. No. I don't get lonely."

"I'm sure I would," said Ashley. That was a lie.

Truth was, Alaska sounded pretty good after the past week—particularly since her professional future was seriously in doubt.

She loved California, but she had to admit, the pace could be grueling. A deserted cabin on a lakeshore in the middle of Alaska with Jordan in front of a roaring fire sounded pretty appealing right now.

"Are you ready to go back?" she asked. Maybe if he took a couple of extra days. Maybe after the Board meeting, they could...

What? She was an L.A. television executive, and he was an Alaskan bush pilot. What good could possibly come of them spending a couple of extra days together?

What exactly did she want from him?

He moved the cart up a few feet. "I'm ready to go back," he answered her question with a nod. "L.A.'s a whole lot of fun. But my bed is in Alaska."

Ashley took a step forward, coming up beside him again. Truth was, she knew exactly what she wanted from him. And it was now or never.

Her stomach began to churn and her palms started to sweat. When she looked up at him, desire and reality crystallized in her mind.

She reached out and placed her hand on his forearm, coming up on her toes and speaking for his ears only. "You want to come back to my place and put dinner off for a while?"

One of his brows arched up in amazement.

"My bed is in California," she said.

7

JORDAN'S HEART dove into an instant free fall.

He'd promised himself he'd keep his hands off Ashley tonight, promised himself he wouldn't proposition her or make any sexual advances. He'd managed fairly well so far, but his teeth were nearly aching with the effort.

But now she said... She wanted...

He glanced at the lineup ahead of them. Three carts to go. Three *full* carts.

He checked out the lineups stretching off to the right. Then those to the left.

Damn.

Why were there only a dozen checkouts open? Didn't these people know that their customers had *things to do?* How the hell was anyone supposed to get out of here?

He supposed ditching the fruit, lifting Ashley into his arms and sprinting for the exit would look way too eager.

"Jordan?"

He wondered wildly if he could bribe the woman in front of them to get the hell out of the way.

"Jordan?"

"Huh?" He stared down at her, blinking.

"I, uh, asked you a question..." A flush crept up on her face. "And you didn't answer—"

"Yes," he cut in, amazed that she couldn't already tell. "The answer is yes, yes, yes."

He reached for her arm, sliding his hand down the length of it, lacing his fingers with hers because he couldn't go another second without touching her. More than anything in the world, he wanted to haul her fully into his arms and press her tight against his body, losing himself in her scent and her feel and her taste.

"Oh." Her flush deepened. "I was afraid—"

He let go of her hand and slipped his arm around her waist, trying to make it look casual, trying to make it look as though they were simply a friendly couple.

"Don't be afraid of anything," he whispered close to her ear.

The checkout clerk handed the first customer his receipt, then she greeted the next person in line. Still two carts to go. Jordan was never going to make it.

"I want you, Ashley," he muttered in her ear. "I *so* want you."

"Price-check on ten," the cashier said into her intercom. "Dumaire's Fine Canned Tuna. Eight-ounce size." Her tinny voice echoed through the store.

"I want you, too," said Ashley, a smile in her voice.

"Jordan. It's 'I want you, Jordan.'"

"I want you, Jordan." She had such a gorgeous voice—and a gorgeous everything else, too.

The cashier scanned a loaf of bread. She scanned it again. Then she sighed and punched in the UPC number by hand.

Jordan glanced back at the other lineups, hoping for a reprieve. The one at the far end seemed to be moving faster. There was a packer down there. But two people had pulled in behind them in this lineup, and he didn't dare move. "Is it always this busy here?" He tried not to sound too desperate.

"Usually."

"Why don't you shop somewhere else?"

"It's close to my apartment."

"Well, thank goodness for that at least." Jordan wasn't sure if he could make a long drive. And he doubted Ashley would be willing to pull over and make love in the back seat halfway home.

The cashier chatted with the customer for a moment, scanned another product, then unrolled a plastic grocery bag and set it up in the stand. Finally, a box boy arrived with her price check.

After some consultation, they came to an agreement, and she rang the tuna through.

She then handed the receipt to the customer, and the woman wheeled her groceries away. Only one more to go. Jordan crowded the final customer with his cart, receiving an annoyed look from the middle-aged woman who was unloading.

The clerk began scanning products in slow motion again.

"Did she go to the cashier school of Tai Chi?" Jordan mumbled under his breath.

"Where?" asked Ashley.

"Never mind. Can you please distract me?"

"What do you mean?"

"I mean I'm nearly going nuts waiting to get you through this lineup and into the car. Say something to distract me."

She pressed tighter against his shoulder, wrapping her fingers around his biceps. "You want me to warm you up or cool you down?" she whispered.

Oh, man. What a choice to have to make.

"Cool me down," he said. "No. Wait... Yeah. Cool me down." Anything else would be suicidal.

"Did you know that statistical research in advertising has recently identified six building blocks of brand equity?" she asked.

"What?"

"They are salience, performance, imagery, judgments, feelings and resonance."

"You are speaking Greek."

"They are used to evaluate a brand's performance and health via the pyramid model."

"Oh, this is seriously working," he said.

"Really?"

"I'm feeling both intimidated and emasculated."

"On second thought," said Ashley, voice lowering, "I am *so* hot for your body."

Jordan stiffened and sucked in a tight breath.

"I'm dying to have you touch me," she continued, "run your fingers over every pulse point, every nerve ending. I'm—"

"Sir?" said the cashier.

Jordan looked up, shaking himself out of a daze.

"Please put your groceries on the conveyor.

"Right."

"How LONG *was* that drive?" Jordan piled the grocery bags on the first available surface—a small table in the entry hall of Ashley's apartment.

"Five minutes," said Ashley, locking the door behind her. "Usually takes me ten."

"Seemed like longer." He turned to face her, lifting her purse out of her hands, discarding it and drawing her into his arms.

She molded against him, as if she was designed exclusively for his body. A small sigh escaped her lips, and his hands convulsed against the small of her back.

"You feel like Heaven," he said, forcing himself to slow down. He'd been humming like an overrevved engine for far too long.

"You feel like sin." She tipped her head back, exposing the delicate skin of her neck.

"In a good way, I hope." He kissed the curve of her

collarbone, suckling, tasting, inhaling deeply. Everything about Ashley was Heaven.

"In a great way," she purred.

His hands made their way under the hem of her shirt, his fingertips scorching on her heat.

She quickly flicked open the buttons of his dress shirt, and then tugged the tails from his waistband.

He started to shake with the need to rip off her clothes and pull her down onto the carpet.

"You want to savor this?" he rasped, balancing on a knife edge of control. "Or you want a slam dunk?"

"Can't I have both?" She pushed his shirt down his arms. It dropped to the floor, and she started on the zipper of his pants.

"In what order?"

"What do you think?" She leaned forward and pressed a kiss in the middle of his chest. Her hot, wet tongue laved the spot as she suckled.

"Thank goodness." He stripped her shirt off and flipped the catch on her bra.

He tugged her against him, skin on skin. Memories of their time on the beach swamped his senses. He slid his hand through her hair to the back of her head, anchoring her firmly while he kissed and kissed, then kissed some more.

Her hands worked on his fly, and his tugged at her skirt.

She made it inside his boxers just as he yanked the skirt down her legs.

He gasped at the touch of her fingers, desire searing a heat trail through his entire body. His hands slipped down and found her, touched her, reveled in her, ratcheting his need past the point of unbearable.

She gasped his name, the entreaty unmistakable. He lowered her to the floor and peeled off her skirt, settling between her legs.

She cupped his face, dark blue eyes penetrating his soul. "Jordan," she gasped.

"Oh, yeah. It's me. Definitely me." He leaned down to kiss her, hard and deep, tasting, breathing, wanting.

Her knees tightened around him.

"You sure?" he forced out.

There was fast, and there was flat-out lightning.

He held his body back by sheer force of will, waiting for her answer. He could feel the sweat popping out on his forehead.

She moved against him. "Yes!"

Thank God.

He pushed inside, and a blinding light went off deep in the base of his brain. His body took over, surging and questing. He knew he should slow down, but primitive hormones were now running the show. Desire pumped through him, obliterating reason.

Ashley moaned, tipping her head back, closing her eyes, fingers convulsing against his shoulders.

He wanted to ask her if she was okay. He wanted to be a gentleman and take care of her. But spots were dancing behind his eyes and he knew he was done for.

Her hands left his shoulders, and gripped his hair. Her breaths came shallow as her head moved from side to side. She groaned his name over and over as the world exploded around him.

ASHLEY SLOWLY became aware of her surroundings.

The whirr of the fan overhead. The buzz of the fridge motor in the kitchen. The rough carpet digging into her rear end. And the delicious warm weight of Jordan all but collapsed on top of her.

"So, which was that?" she gasped.

"Hmm?" He rolled onto his back, taking her with him so that she was cradled against his naked body.

"Was that savoring or the slam dunk?"

She felt his laughter rumble deep in his chest. He reached up and brushed a lock of hair out of her eyes, placing a gentle kiss on her temple. "If that was savoring, you'd better kick me out now."

"You're not going anywhere." If she could figure a way to lock him up in her apartment for a month or so, she'd do it.

"I'm not?"

"Not until you help me eat all that expensive fruit you bought. Should I make the salad?"

"You mean to tell me you can actually move?"

"You mean to tell me that's all you have in you?"

He quickly rolled over, pinning her to the floor again. "Not hardly." His hand went to her breast, fingertips rolling her nipple.

"Good." She sucked in a breath as streaks of desire radiated out from his caress. She fought the urge to kiss him now and start all over again. "You can peel the kiwis."

"You drive a hard bargain," he said.

"Yeah? Well you drive a hard—" She broke off the sentence, chickening out.

Jordan grinned. "Hold that thought." He levered off her and lifted the grocery bags. "I'll peel the kiwis if you wash the strawberries. I have a feeling I'm going to need my strength."

While Jordan headed for the kitchen, Ashley sat up. His dress shirt was piled in a heap on the floor beside her, so she slipped her arms in the sleeves and wrapped it around her body.

She padded barefoot onto the cool linoleum.

Jordan turned to look at her.

"Nice..." he said, slowly dragging his gaze from her head to her toes, a wolfish grin appearing on his face. "I have no idea why Jeffrey calls you the iron maiden." He pulled a sharp knife from the butcher block on her counter.

"The what?" she asked.

"The iron maiden. You must not be near as nice to him as you are to me."

"You obviously don't know your brother very well." She crossed the kitchen and took the strawberries out of the bag.

"I don't know him at all." Jordan removed the kiwi peel in one long, curly strand.

"Well, he's not as nice as you."

He cut off a slice of green kiwi and held it to her lips. "Doesn't surprise me. Few people are. Here. Try some."

"There goes that ego again."

"Doesn't mean it's not true."

He had a point. Ashley smiled as she opened her mouth. The moist, sweet fruit slid across her tongue. "Mmm," she murmured.

Jordan sliced off another piece and ate it himself. Then he leaned forward and gave her a lingering kiss.

He split the final half of the kiwi, placing one piece in her mouth, the other in his. Then he set the knife down.

She swallowed, and he smiled, taking his juice-covered fingertip and drawing a leisurely circle over her lips. Her nerve endings pulsed, and he slowly pushed the fingertip into her mouth. She curled her tongue around it, desire tickling its way through her body.

"Strawberries next." He kissed the corner of her mouth, slowly withdrawing his finger. "Then we'll talk peaches."

"This could take a long time," she sighed.

"The longer the better," said Jordan. "This is the savoring part."

JORDAN AWOKE with Ashley nestled tightly in his arms, spoon fashion. Her soft bottom was pressed against his stomach and he could smell the sweet scent of her hair.

He placed a gentle kiss behind one ear.

"What time is it?" she muttered.

"Early," he whispered back.

She shifted against him, and he felt a slow, heady arousal drift through his body.

"We have to go to work," she sighed.

"Not yet."

"I promised Rob I'd meet him for the storyboards."

Jordan trailed his hand across her stomach. Her skin was toasty warm from sleep, and it was soft against weather-worn fingertips. "You okay with all this?"

There was a smile in her voice. "You might have to be a little more specific with that question."

"Helping me. Helping Jeffrey with the promotion. I have to tell you, I'm feeling a little guilty about it all."

She shifted onto her back so she could look him in the eyes. Hers were midnight-blue, reflecting the early light that filtered through her pale curtains. "I thought you were talking about making love."

He smoothed her tousled hair back from her forehead, enjoying the silky feel. "I'm no fool. I'll just assume you're fine with *that* until you tell me otherwise."

She smiled, and he couldn't resist pulling her forward for a kiss.

Her lips heated under his, and the kiss quickly deepened. As sexual energy recharged his system, he felt an edge of desperation creep in. He was leaving her in twenty-four hours. His arm tightened around her waist.

How was he going to do that?

When he realized she could barely breathe, he forced himself to pull back. "You're gorgeous in the morning."

"So are you."

He trailed a fingertip between her breasts. "Do you think we have time..."

She shook her head. "Not unless you can shave about ten minutes off last night's record."

He squelched his disappointment. "I don't think that's possible. And I don't think you'd want me to."

She started to sit up. "I guess that's true."

But he put a hand on her shoulder and pinned her gently to the bed. "No so fast. We must at least have time for another kiss."

She sank back into the pillow. "You don't think that might be a little dangerous?"

"Danger is my middle name."

She laughed softly, as he wrapped his arms around her, rolling onto his back, pulling her with him so that she pressed him into the mattress. "You feel *so* good."

She sighed, peppering mini kisses along his collarbone. "I wish we could hide out here forever."

He buried his face in her hair, inhaling and planting a gentle kiss on her soft crown. "We can."

She smiled against his chest. "But then Carl would win."

"Who'd care? We'd be here making love for the rest of our lives."

She propped herself up, shaking her hair out of her eyes and digging her elbows into his chest for support.

It wasn't the most comfortable position in the world, but he wasn't about to complain.

"Jeffrey would care," she said.

Her radio alarm clicked on, and the sounds of soft rock filled her bedroom.

"You're my brother's guardian angel now?"

She shook her head. "I'd care, too. And the other employees would care. Carl's bad news for Argonaut. He might push up the ratings in the short term, but we'd lose good people with him around."

"So, you're really okay with this?"

She shrugged. "No. I'm not okay with it. I hate it. I hate that I'm not getting a chance at that job. And I hate that I'm helping to get it for Jeffrey. It's not right and it's not fair."

Jordan tightened him arms around the small of her back. He wanted to hold her close and protect her from everything the world wanted to dish out. But, even if she was the kind of woman who needed protection, this was way beyond his power to control.

"Sometimes I hate this whole business," she said.

That surprised him. "Really? It seemed like you were having a lot of fun on the video clip shoots yesterday."

She nodded. "I like developing new projects. I've always loved the shoots. It's the office politics that are hard to take. The push and shove and attack and betrayal..."

Now Jordan was really confused. "Then why are you trying so hard to get to the top?"

"Because it's the top."

"But, if you like working on the sets, why not work on the sets?"

"Working on the sets is where you start. It's not where you end up."

"But if that's where your—"

"You're starting to sound like my father."

"How so?"

She dropped her voice an octave, obviously mimicking her father's tone. "Don't set your sights too high, Ashley. It's a tough world out there. Remember there's pride in any job you take on."

"That's good advice."

"Yeah? If there's pride in any job, then why does he brag so much about my brother's expanding law firm and my other brother's million-dollar electronics company?" She shook her head. "No, a middle-of-the-road job isn't okay for his sons, only for his daughter."

"I have a middle-of-the-road job."

"Really?"

"My airline's not so big."

She laid her head down on his chest, and snuggled against his side. "Tell me about your life in Alaska."

"Aren't we going to be late?"

"I'll shower fast."

"Okay. Alaska. It's wild. It's cold. It's beautiful. But it's pretty slow-paced compared to here."

"Slow-paced sounds nice to me right now." Her breath puffed against his skin, and the song on the radio switched to a romantic ballad.

He stroked her hair again. This time, sifting it between his fingers, watching it glitter like gold in the early morning light. "I live in a little cabin in the Alaska bush. It's on the shore of Glacier Lake, ten miles from Alpine."

"Do you have any neighbors?"

"About a dozen. The closest is a quarter of a mile down the lakeshore."

"Is there a beach?"

"Yeah. Miles of white sand, but it's too cold to swim most of the year. In fact, the water's only open for six months at a stretch."

"How cold is it?"

"The water?"

"The weather."

"We usually hit forty below for part of every winter."

She shivered. "I'd freeze."

"I have a great woodstove."

"No electricity?"

"A generator. But I only run it when I need it."

"What about plumbing?"

"A well. And, yes, it flows out of taps inside the cabin. I have a gas-powered water pump and a propane water heater. And there's a satellite dish on a tree out back. It's really very civilized."

"You live alone?"

"I do."

She trailed her fingertips across his chest, down onto his stomach, dipping into the indentation of his navel. Her voice dropped. "You have a girlfriend up there?"

His hand on her hair stilled. "If I did, I wouldn't be here."

She nodded.

They were both silent for a moment.

She shifted. "I didn't mean..."

"I know. It's okay." Fidelity sure couldn't be taken for granted these days.

"What about your business?" she asked.

"My airline has six bush planes. We mostly service south-eastern Alaska, but we also fly up to the North Slope and out on the Kenai."

She walked her fingers up his chest again, distracting him. "How many people work for you?"

He stilled her hand. "Ten pilots and half a dozen ground crew. If you don't stop that, we're definitely going to be late."

She smiled, but didn't stop teasing him with her touches. "Do you fly?"

"Not so much anymore."

She lifted her head to look at him again. "Would you like to?"

Good question. Some days he missed flying. In fact, lots of days he missed flying. "I guess I would."

Her smile widened. "Will you take me flying sometime?"

"Anytime, anywhere," he said solemnly.

Her expression turned serious again, and she leaned in for a kiss.

He cupped her face in his hand and curled his tongue around hers.

After long minutes, she broke away. There was a catch in her voice. "We have to go."

He sighed. "I know."

She gave him a brave smile. "The big, bad world awaits."

He kissed the tip of her nose. "Let's go get 'em, tiger."

8

MEMORIES OF Ashley still flitting through his mind, Jordan headed into Jeffrey's office to start his final workday. To his shock, Carl was sitting at his meeting table, casually perusing a computer printout.

He didn't even bother looking up when Jordan walked in. "*Hello Hildy* hit thirty-four last week," he said.

Jordan stopped in his tracks, instantly wary. He knew *Hello Hildy* was an after-school children's show, but there his knowledge stopped. He didn't know if a thirty-four was good, bad or neutral.

After a moment's silence, Carl glanced up, eyebrows raised, obviously waiting for an answer.

Despite his apprehension, Jordan felt a sense of annoyance. The man had a lot of nerve invading his office. If Jordan wasn't in such a precarious position, he'd demand to know what Carl thought he was doing.

But he could hardly get antagonistic and confrontational with somebody who could potentially blow his cover.

"I see," said Jordan, without inflection. Staying

noncommittal seemed like the safest course of action. At the same time, he watched Carl closely for signs that he'd figured out the deception.

"Happy about that?" asked Carl.

The question seemed merely conversational. And Jordan felt a bit of the tension drain out of him. Apparently he wasn't caught, yet. But he sure wished he knew whether a thirty-four was something to celebrate or something to worry about.

"Some people would be, I guess," he tried carefully.

Carl unexpectedly grinned. "A man after my own heart."

Jordan smiled coldly in return. Carl might think they'd found some common ground, but Jordan's opinion of the man wasn't about to change.

He walked behind his desk, hoping to keep this conversation short and sweet. "What can I do for you, Carl?"

Carl slouched back in the chair. He seemed to be studying Jordan, gauging him somehow. And, despite his dispassionate expression, his fingers twitched against the cover of the computer report. "I think you and I may be in a position to help each other."

Jordan's senses went on alert.

"I figure we're both intelligent, practical men," said Carl.

Jordan didn't say a word, figuring he'd get himself in a lot less trouble by staying silent.

"We both know how this town works. We both

know how to get things done." Carl paused, giving Jordan an opportunity to jump in.

But Jordan wasn't jumping anywhere.

"I have to say, I appreciated you watching my ass on the Verona deal." This time, Carl hit Jordan with a significant, questioning look.

It was obvious Jordan was going to have to respond. His mind scrambled for a logical response. If he made Carl suspicious, he was in serious trouble. But, what was Verona, and why would his brother have any dealings at *all* with a man like Carl?

The only scrap of relevant information he could come up with, was that it must have happened while Jeffrey was still in California. At least a year ago.

He shrugged carelessly, tossing his Q-23 clipboard down on his desktop, and easing into his chair. "No problem. Water under the bridge."

Carl's smile broadened. It turned slick and serpentine, making Jordan nervous.

Carl's twitchy fingers stilled, and his eyes widened with speculation. "Are you telling me you saw the advantage of Verona?"

Jordan didn't see any choice but to play along. He shrugged again. "Sure. Why not?"

Carl chuckled and shook his head. "I can see New York was good for you."

Jordan raised his eyebrows.

"It obviously helped you put things in perspective. I like that."

Jordan really couldn't care less what Carl liked or didn't like. He just wanted the man to get the heck out of his office. Better still, he wanted him to get the heck out of his and Ashley's lives.

He wasn't sure how much longer he could keep up this cat and mouse conversation. All it would take was one wrong answer for Carl to catch on to the fact that he was bluffing.

"I think I pretty much have things in perspective," he said, struggling to keep the irony out of his voice.

Carl straightened in the chair, shifting to face Jordan fully. "Then I guess you've figured out that I've been planning this move for a very long time."

What move? "Of course."

Carl's expression turned reflective. "Everything had to be in place. The right people had to be on board. You know this town. You move too soon, it'll fall down on you like a house of cards."

Jordan took another stab at sounding coherent. "You obviously made some smart moves while I was away."

Carl tapped his index finger against the plastic printout cover. His eyes narrowed. "If I'd known you felt this way, I would have asked you to wait in New York."

Jordan's shoulders tensed up. Why wouldn't Carl just leave? The situation was getting less and less bluffable by the minute. "Would that have helped?"

Carl's voice rose. "Of course it would have helped. You being here complicates the whole process."

Jordan had talked himself into a corner. Carl and Jeffrey obviously had a complex history that was about to rear up and bite Jordan in the butt.

Would it have *killed* Jeffrey to give him a little more information on this?

He was quickly running out of noncommittal answers here. "That's true,"

Carl leaned back, lifting his arms, lacing his fingers behind his head. "So, are you going to waste a whole lot of time playing hardball, or will you agree up front to get out of my way?"

Jordan picked up his pen and tapped it against the desktop a couple of times, stalling. How the hell did he answer that one?

Getting out of Carl's way had to be about the vice president's job. Nothing else made sense.

But why? *Why* would Jeffrey agree to blow the promotion for Carl? From their radio conversations in Alpine, it was painfully obvious that this promotion was important to Jeffrey.

"I'm prepared to offer you a cut of course," Carl elaborated.

Oh, great. Now he was being bribed.

Now what? Did he agree? Did he tell Carl to take a flying leap?

Carl watched Jordan's indecision from beneath hooded eyes.

"Define cut," Jordan finally answered.

Carl smiled broadly and nodded in satisfaction. "Glad to know you've seen the light. Though, I have to admit, I'm a little surprised."

Jordan figured there was nothing to do but go all the way on this. He might as well let Carl think he was a mercenary. "I don't know why you would be. A guy's got to look after his own interests."

"I'm glad we understand each other."

"I think we do," said Jordan. He was pretty darn sure he had a handle on what kind of man Carl was.

Carl stood up and straightened his jacket, lifting his chin in a posture of supreme confidence. "It's settled then. Ashley's already bowed out. Not that she was a serious threat. We both know she's a nonstarter. A nice piece of ass, but a nonstarter."

Jordan dropped his hands beneath the desk, clenching his fists, quelling the instantaneous urge to tear Carl's head off.

Oblivious to the effect of his words, Carl headed for the door. He stopped with his hand on the knob, turning to face Jordan. "There's no need to cut her in on the deal. But we can keep her around if you want. For whatever."

"Right," said Jordan tightly. If Carl wanted to live, he'd better be gone in the next ten seconds.

"And, tomorrow. You know. Don't make it look too obvious, hmmm?"

Jordan had no intention of blowing tomorrow's job

interview in favor of Carl. There was no way in the world he'd leave this bottom feeder as Ashley's boss. As soon as he could reach Jeffrey, he was getting some answers. Then he was coming after Carl with guns blazing.

He stood up and tossed the pen down on the desk. "Just so I'm clear. My cut is..."

Carl laughed and shook his head. "New York really was good for you." He sobered. "It's the same deal I had at Fifth Dimension. You get the title of senior acquisitions director and twenty-five percent of my take."

Jordan nodded, his skin practically crawling as Carl left the office. Whatever the "take" was, it couldn't be legal.

As soon as the door shut, he reached for the phone. Jeffrey had a whole lot of explaining to do.

But as his hand touched the receiver, a suspicion flashed through his mind. He yanked back.

Carl didn't strike him as a stupid man. Obnoxious and dishonest, yes. But definitely not stupid. And he'd have to be pretty stupid to trust Jordan this fast.

Jordan stepped quietly across the carpet to the office door. He silently cracked it open.

Bingo.

There was Carl, standing right outside the office, making small talk with Bonnie, and glancing at her phone every ten seconds, obviously checking to see if Jordan's line lit up.

Jordan watched and waited.

Two minutes passed. Then five. Then finally, Carl left.

Jordan started to withdraw, but then he noticed the computer report still sitting on Bonnie's desk.

Sure enough. Carl slithered back in. Using the forgotten report as a ruse, he glanced at the phone again. Then he smiled in satisfaction and left the outer office.

Jordan quietly closed the door and headed back to his own desk.

What kind of business *was* this?

He picked up the phone and tried to connect with the Mush Lodge. The operator did her best, but the snowstorm had taken out one of the radio towers, and the signal was too weak to go through.

Next, he tried Ashley's office number.

"Ashley Baines," she answered.

"Is Rob still with you? Are you alone?"

Her voice dropped to a sultry whisper. "I'm all alone."

"Is your office door closed?"

"Why? You want me to get naked?"

"No."

"No?"

"Later."

"Okay."

"I just talked with Carl Nedesco."

Her voice instantly returned to normal. "About what?"

"I'm not sure." He took a breath. "Okay, maybe I am sure. He just bribed me to throw the vice president's job."

"He *what?*"

"He offered me senior acquisitions director and twenty-five percent of his take. What does that mean?"

"It means he's a whole lot more afraid of you than he is of me."

She had that right—unfounded though Carl's chauvinistic, ignorant opinion might be. The man had completely dismissed Ashley. Of course, there was no way in the world Jordan would *ever* share that part of the conversation with her.

Ashley's voice turned worried. "What did you say to him? Did he guess you weren't Jeffrey?"

"No. He didn't know. I'm positive of that."

"Thank goodness."

"I let him think I was interested in taking the bribe. I was trying to figure out what he was up to without giving myself away. Does the name *Verona* mean anything to you?"

There was a silence on Ashley's end of the line.

"Ashley?"

"I'm coming down there *right* now."

"No! Don't. I think he's spying on me. He waited in my outer office for about ten minutes to see if I'd pick up the phone. I'm sure he's going to be watching what

I do and who I see for the rest of the day. You stay away."

"We need to meet," she said.

"I know."

"Away from the office."

"Definitely."

"Okay," she said. "I agree that you probably shouldn't rush out right now. How about this? I told Rob we'd shoot the café scene at one. You remember how to get to the Green Onion?"

"I do."

"Good. We can talk after the shoot."

"Ashley?"

"What?"

"Is your life always like this?"

She paused. "Not always."

"This business you're in is nuts, you know that?"

IT WAS THREE O'CLOCK at the Green Onion Café before Ashley had a chance to talk to Jordan alone. She'd waited on pins and needles throughout the shoot.

Anything Carl Nedesco was involved with, couldn't be good. And Verona Productions was serious bad news. Jordan had to stay well away from anyone who'd had anything to do with Verona.

As soon as the last crew member left, she latched on to Jordan and dragged him to a corner table, ducking under an old fisherman's net and an antique lantern that were suspended from rough-hewn beams.

She plunked down on the worn wooden chair, and he took the one opposite.

"Tell me everything Carl said about Verona Productions," she prompted.

Jordan glanced around to make sure they weren't being overheard, then he moderated his voice. "He thanked me for 'watching his ass' on the Verona deal. Then he said if he'd known I'd support him he would have asked me to wait in New York."

"Support him on what?"

Jordan shrugged. "Whatever scam he's cooked up. I didn't get details. But definitely something to do with money. He talked about 'the take,' remember?"

Ashley lifted her hand to her mouth, biting down on her thumbnail. The clatter from the kitchen and the conversations from other tables ebbed and flowed around them while she tried to make sense of the situation.

Try as she might, she couldn't imagine why Jeffrey would have had anything to do with Carl. "Did he say that Jeffrey had already made a deal with him?"

Jordan shook his head. "No. In fact, he seemed surprised that I would go along."

Okay, that sounded a little bit more like Jeffrey. So, why would Carl approach Jeffrey in the first place?

"He must be really worried about you beating him," she ventured. "It was a big risk for him to come to you."

"You mean he's worried about Jeffrey beating him," said Jordan.

"Right," Ashley agreed. Jordan wasn't Jeffrey, and that was getting to be a bigger and bigger problem all the time.

A waitress approached the table, plunking down glasses of ice water and handing them both giant menus with bright pictures of fish swimming around on the front.

"He was very cautious," said Jordan over the top of the big, plastic folder. "He felt me out at first, talking in generalities. It was all very obtuse and cagey."

Ashley set her menu down across her silverware. She needed to figure out what Carl was up to. "Tell me everything you remember. Exactly."

"Are you eating?" asked Jordan.

"I'll have a salad."

Jordan set down his own menu. "Carl said 'everything was in place,' and 'the right people were on board,' and he wanted to know if I was going to agree or play hardball."

"And what did you say?"

"I asked him what was in it for me."

"And?"

"That was when he told me senior acquisitions director and twenty-five percent of his take."

Ashley's stomach clenched. She gripped her glass of ice water, dropping her voice to a whisper. She didn't like this. Not one little bit. "And he mentioned Verona Productions."

"Right."

It was even worse than Ashley had thought. If Carl became vice president, the same unsavory elements that conceived Verona were going to get a toehold in Argonaut.

She ran her fingertip through the condensation on her glass. "Six years ago, the owners of Verona were convicted of bribery. It seems they paid off studio executives to push their shows. There was evidence of money laundering, unsavory connections. It got ugly."

Jordan looked incredulous. "Are you telling me my brother was involved in something illegal?"

"No." Ashley shook her head. She didn't mean that at all. "The people involved went to trial. But lots of other people in the industry knew about the scam. Some knew more than others."

"You think Jeffrey knew something?"

"He must have suspected something about Carl," she explained. "And he must have been right."

Jordan's jaw clenched.

"I'm sure he would have come forward if he'd had solid evidence," said Ashley. Jeffrey was tough as nails. But he wasn't a criminal.

She offered Jordan a half smile. "If nothing else, your brother's got way too much pride to earn money by committing a crime."

"But, because he kept quiet, Carl's assumption is that Jeffrey is crooked."

"Carl superimposes his own standards on the rest of the world. Because he's greedy and immoral, he thinks we're all greedy and immoral."

"Plus, I just took a bribe from the jerk." Jordan shook his head. "That was real helpful to my brother."

Ashley could understand Jordan's growing anger. She wished she had the power to stop Carl. It was bad enough when he was lurking in the periphery of her life at industry functions. She couldn't stand the thought of having him invade her company.

"Explain to me how a guy like that starts climbing the corporate ladder in the first place," Jordan demanded. "Don't any of their executives *see* what he's like?"

Sad as it was, guys like Carl were pretty common in L.A. "Lowlifes make a lot of money for the studios."

"Nice business you're in."

Ashley stopped herself from reacting to the insult. Jordan was upset. She didn't blame him. She was upset, too.

"Backroom deals are not confined to Hollywood," she pointed out.

"I think this is a little more than a backroom deal."

True enough. But there were guys like Carl everywhere. She was willing to bet there were even a few of them in the Alaskan aviation industry. But, she kept her mouth shut on that score.

Jordan took a swig of his ice water. "It goes without saying that I'm not blowing the promotion for Carl."

"Of course not. You still need to win."

"Do you think Carl's involved with Verona again?"

"He can't be. Verona doesn't exist. The company went bankrupt."

Jordan's brows knit together. "Then, what's this about?"

Unfortunately, it didn't take a rocket scientist to figure that one out. Senior acquisitions director? Twenty-five percent of the take? The right people in the right places?

"Carl's found another crooked production company," she said. "And he's planning to set up the same scam at Argonaut."

Jordan plunked the glass back down on the table. "Well, he's not going to get away with it."

"Not if you win the promotion. Then he goes away with his tail between his legs." Ashley would work round the clock to make sure that happened.

Jordan shook his head. "Oh, no."

She felt a shimmer of apprehension. "What do you mean, no?"

"I'm not going up against Carl. It's too big a risk."

The shimmer was turning into full-blown panic. "But, it's our only hope."

"I'm going to the Board."

"You can't do that." Bad move. Very, very bad move.

"Of course I can. I'm not going to let Carl get away with this."

"They won't believe you."

"Why not?"

Her voice rose. "Because you and I both have something to gain by discrediting Carl."

Jordan looked completely affronted. "I'd never make up a crime to discredit someone."

Ashley felt a surge of frustration build within her. A little Alaskan naiveté was cute in the grocery store, but surely Jordan wasn't that innocent. "You know that, and I know that, but they—"

"I'm sure they're perfectly reasonable people," Jordan said with a confidence that discounted her opinion completely.

"They're perfectly experienced and jaded people. You go in there with unfounded allegations—"

"They're not unfounded."

"It's your word against his. You have no proof—"

He reached out and covered her hand. "Ashley."

Ashley gritted her teeth and yanked her hand away. He might as well have patted her on the head and told her not to strain her pretty little brain over this. Him, the big, bad male in the conversation knew what was best.

"If Carl beats me, Jeffrey will be a criminal."

"Jeffrey won't take the money," said Ashley.

"Which will make him Carl's enemy. And what

about you? What about the other employees. Do you *want* Carl to get the job?"

"Why are you patronizing me?"

Jordan drew back. "Excuse me?"

"Has it occurred to you that I might know a little bit more about this business than you?"

"I'm not allowed to have an opinion?"

"I'm telling you that going to the Board is the *worst* thing you can do right now." They didn't have a shred of evidence, and Carl would have hidden his tracks well.

Jordan's eyes went cold. "And I'm telling you that going to the Board is the *only* thing I can do right now."

"You'll hand the vice presidency to Carl on a silver platter." Ashley knew this with a concrete certainty.

"In your opinion."

"Which doesn't appear to count for anything."

Jordan opened his mouth. Then he closed it again. The noise in the restaurant seemed to rise, suffocating Ashley as fear started to rise within her. She wasn't going to win this argument.

Finally, Jordan spoke. "Going to the Board is the only alternative that protects Jeffrey."

Ashley clenched her fists. "You winning is the only alternative that protects Jeffrey."

Jordan shook his head. "No. That's a serious long shot, and I'm not willing to gamble with my brother's future."

She tried reason one last time. "Trying for the promotion might be a gamble, but going to the Board is a sure thing. It's a sure thing that Carl will beat us."

Jordan stared into her eyes for a moment, then focused on a spot behind her. "I don't see it that way."

"Well, you're wrong."

Her flat words hung in the air for a moment before he swung his focus back to her eyes and spoke. "I don't think so."

"Don't do it, Jordan."

"I have to protect my brother."

A chill of dread shot up Ashley's spine. "I know this game better than you do."

He stood up. "I can't risk it."

"Jordan..."

He shook his head, and walked out of the café.

9

IT WAS AFTER ten that night when Jordan finally made it to the screening room. He wasn't sure if he'd find Ashley there or not. Earlier, they'd agreed to view the rest of the pilots late in the day, in order to avoid Carl. But, in the hours since their argument, he hadn't called her, and she hadn't called him.

He wasn't completely sure they were speaking to each other.

He'd spent the afternoon examining the Carl question from all angles. Unfortunately, he was no closer to an answer now than he had been when he walked out of the café. There were just too many unknown factors.

If Ashley was right, and Harold Gauthier thought he'd made up the accusations in order to discredit Carl, Carl would find out, and it would ruin Jeffrey's career. But, if he waited, and Carl got the vice president's job, he would put Jeffrey in an untenable position.

Jeffrey deserved to have his opinion heard on this. And Jordan had tried to get hold of his brother, but it looked like there wouldn't be any radio communica-

tion between here and Katimuk for some time
to come.

He pushed open the screening room door.

Ashley turned her head from where she was sitting
facing the blank screen. "I'm surprised you bothered
to come." Her voice was anything but welcoming.

"We've still got work to do," he responded, striding
to the row of big chairs where she sat prim and still.

"Not if you're going to chuck it all by going to Harold Gauthier," she snapped.

Nice. This was certainly going to be pleasant.

He sat down in the same row, leaving an empty seat
between them. "I haven't decided anything yet."

"Well, do let us peons know once you've made up
your mind."

Jordan ignored the dig. He was way too tired to argue. "What's up first?"

He could feel her glare for a few moments before
she clicked the remote control.

"Blue Heat," she said tersely. "A cop show."

As the opening credits rolled, she started writing,
her pen flying over the page with bold strokes, her anger almost palpable in the dim room.

Jordan waited patiently a few minutes while the
primary characters were introduced in a short scene at
a police station.

"You going to explain to me how you're dissecting
it, or should I just wing it tomorrow?" he asked, some
of his pent-up frustration showing through. He knew

approximately five percent of what he might need to-morrow.

"Does that mean you're going to give the promotion a shot?" she asked, her attention flicking between the unfolding drama on the screen and the form on the clipboard in front of her.

"I told you, haven't decided yet."

She quickly pressed down on the pause button, and turned to glare at him. "Well, forgive me if I'm tired of busting my ass for a guy who's going to throw it all away because he won't take advice from a woman."

Jordan couldn't believe she'd said that. "Whoa. Who said any of this has to do with you being a woman?"

"Are you trying to tell me you'd be so quick to dismiss my advice if I was a man?"

He felt as if he'd been blindsided. "How come I never noticed that huge chip on your shoulder before?"

"Because you were too busy staring at my breasts."

The muscles in his neck grew taut. "That wasn't fair."

She shook her head and laughed darkly. "This is Hollywood, Jordan. Nothing's fair."

Jordan sighed. "We do *not* have time to do this."

He picked up the remote control and hit the play button. "Just tell me how you're analyzing this. We'll have to fight later."

"There's not going to be any later," she muttered under her breath.

"I heard that."

"I know."

Jordan pointed to the screen. "What are you writing about him?"

Ashley was silent.

For a minute there he didn't think she was going to answer.

"He's the sidekick," she finally said, some of the energy draining out of her voice. "If this pilot is done well, he should also be a foil for the male lead. See the books behind him? He's an intellectual where the lead character is a street scrapper. I'll watch to see if the scriptwriter uses that later."

Jordan leaned forward as the action heated up. A villain lurked in the background of a dark warehouse where the hero was undercover.

A woman came on screen. "Love interest," said Ashley. "Again, if it's done right, she's everything he can't have, everything that threatens his sense of self. And, see that? See how he lost his temper when he should have kept cool. That's his fatal flaw."

She made some notes on the form. "Whoever wrote this knew what they were doing."

Jordan found himself getting caught up with the story of a cop so deep undercover that he began to lose his bearings. Even with Ashley's curt monologue on the set, the script and the special effects, he found the story fascinating.

When the ending credits ran, he whistled low. "That's gotta be a keeper."

"Yeah. We definitely won't send that to the vaults."

He raised his eyebrows. "The vaults?"

She didn't look at him. "It's where old pilots go when they die."

"As an old pilot, I don't particularly like the sound of that."

He hoped to get a smile out of her, but she wasn't biting. She simply queued up the next program.

It was a pop music show. Jordan thought it was pretty mediocre, and Ashley seemed to agree. Even accounting for the fact that he didn't care for hip-hop, the show really dragged.

Jordan didn't try any more jokes while she queued up the final pilot episode. It was described as a late-night talk show, titled *In And Out.*

As the tape started to roll, the lights came up on a set that looked like a middle-class living room. A large impressionist mural of a sunset hung behind a love seat and two brown, leather wingback chairs. The carpet was cream-colored, the lighting soft.

A gray-haired woman walked onto the stage, pausing to acknowledge the applause of a small studio audience before she stepped onto the dais.

"Welcome," she said as she sat down in one of the wingback chairs and adjusted her navy dress over her knees. "Thank you so much for joining us tonight. I'm Marion Hanson, and this is *In And Out.* The show where we talk frankly about intimacy, relationships and sexuality."

Jordan felt his eyes go wide. He snuck a sideways glance at Ashley, but she was writing notes, not reacting to the unusual subject matter.

Sixty-year-old Marion Hanson smiled benignly into the camera. She folded her hands in her lap, and Jordan fully expected her to recite a chocolate-chip cookie recipe.

"Tonight's topic is orgasms," she said, amazing Jordan even further. "The physiology, the psychology, societal views and, most importantly..." Her eyes twinkled. "How to achieve *really* good ones."

Jordan shifted in his chair as he remembered his last *really good one* with Ashley. He suddenly wished they weren't fighting. He wanted to toss over a one-liner. And he wanted to laugh with her again.

On screen, Marion turned serious and leaned toward the camera. "Now, I know some of you won't have had one in a very long time. And perhaps you're feeling a little frustrated, a little disappointed."

Jordan snuck another sideways glance at Ashley, wishing he could make a joke about *not* being disappointed. Ashley rocked his world.

He covertly watched Ashley as Marion continued on in the background. "Well, I'm happy to tell you that we have a few tips and tricks to share with you tonight that might just get you back on track to the sweet, blissful, overwhelming experience that every human being longs for. Our first guest tonight is Doctor Stephen Reynolds. He's a researcher from..."

Finally, Jordan couldn't stand sitting in stony-faced silence any longer. He just wanted to talk to her. He leaned over. "Uh, Ashley?"

"Hmmm?"

"Are you going to tell me what you're writing?"

She glanced up at him, looking annoyed. "I just wrote that their description of the blue one was a little flat."

"The blue..." Jordan followed her gaze back to the television where, good grief, Marion and the doctor were whipping out a series of brightly colored adult "toys" and expounding on their uses and capabilities.

"Oh," said Jordan.

"They should at least try to make it sound appealing."

Jordan couldn't say the blue one looked particularly appealing to him. But at least it got her talking.

Marion moved onto the orange one, and Jordan tipped his head sideways trying to picture...

"Uh, Ashley?"

"Yeah?"

"Don't you find this show a little out there?"

"How do you mean?"

"Out there, as in my grandmother is on television giving out sex advice."

"Is that your grandmother?" He was sure he heard a smile in her voice that time.

Some of the tension left his body and he sighed in relief.

"Does this stuff actually go on the air?" he asked to keep the conversation going.

"Not this one. It's not particularly original—"

"It's *not*?" Jordan gestured to the screen in amazement, where Marion had wheeled in a whiteboard and a box of colored felt pens. "There's a blue-haired lady drawing a picture of a sexual position I haven't even heard of."

Ashley considered the drawing. "Do you think that's anatomically possible?"

"Not unless you're a circus performer. Who comes up with this stuff?"

"Flexible ladies with lots of experience?"

"You have to talk to your partner," Marion said into the camera.

She rubbed a bright green toy in the palm of her hand. "That's very important. Ask her if you're thrusting too hard. Or perhaps she likes it faster. Or maybe slower. Or—and you may have heard this from some of your patients, Doctor—maybe she'd like you to put your—"

"Ashley?"

"Hmmm?"

"Do I have to sit in a room full of men tomorrow morning and talk about this show?"

"Of course." She kept writing.

"Shoot me now."

"It won't kill you. Just read my notes."

Oh, yeah, Jordan couldn't wait to do that.

"Now, keep quiet and watch," she said. "I'm exhausted. I just want to finish these up so you can copy them out."

Fifteen minutes later, Ashley turned off the television.

Jordan had to admit, he'd learned a few things—nothing he'd ever use, quite frankly. But it was definitely an education.

Ashley set down the remote and stretched her neck to the right and to the left. She looked even more exhausted than Jordan felt.

He felt a renewed rush of guilt over all the hard work she was putting in. Particularly when he might not even be able to use it.

He got up from his chair and crossed to hers. "Come on, let's go."

She shook her head. "I have to finish your presentation. The café scene isn't edited, and the storyboards aren't ready yet. That is…" She looked up at him, eyes narrowing. "If you're planning to present it tomorrow."

"I don't know," Jordan whispered honestly.

He *had* to make the right choice here. But he simply didn't know yet what the right choice was.

She was staring at him, hard. "Remember how you

said not taking my advice had nothing to do with my being a woman?"

"It doesn't."

"Think about this. If we were flying through a blizzard in Alaska and you wanted to land the plane, and I suggested we keep going, would you do it my way?"

The analogy made Jordan pause.

"Would you even *consider* taking my advice under those circumstances? When you have years of training and experience under your belt and I'm simply offering an uninformed opinion?

"All I'm asking," she said, "is that you remember I'*m* the expert here. I'm sure if I was a man you'd have a lot less trouble."

Would he?

Jordan didn't honestly know.

"This is different," he said. "It's not hypothetical, and there's so much at stake."

She sighed and stood up. "And there wouldn't be so much at stake in an airplane?"

Jordan couldn't answer that. He had to think, but he was too tired to think. So was she?

"Your place is closer," he said. "You can finish up the presentation there while I write the new Q-23s."

THE HOME COMPUTER screen blurred in front of Ashley's eyes.

Five more minutes, she told herself. Anybody could stay awake for five more minutes. She just had to...

"Ashley?" Jordan's voice was close to her ear, and she felt his warm breath on her neck.

"Hmmm." Something was digging into her cheek.

"I think you killed the mouse."

"Huh?"

"You're asleep on your desk," he whispered. "Come on." His arm tightened around her shoulders.

She shook her head. "I have to read—"

"You're all done, babe." He gently but firmly lifted her to her feet, and her skin tingled where he touched her. "Time to go to bed."

"But, I'm not finished."

"You need to get some sleep. Whatever we've got right now, we're going with tomorrow." He started leading her away from her desk.

Ashley blinked, trying to orient herself as they headed into the hall. She wished they weren't fighting. His strong arms felt so good around her, and when he talked to her in that low sexy voice, like he cared that she was tired, like she mattered to him...

He'd flipped off the lights as they passed, until only a glow from the entryway shone on her hardwood floor.

"Did you finish the Q-23s?" she asked, letting herself lean into him just a little bit. Surely that wouldn't hurt.

"All done," he said close to her ear.

The timbre of his voice reverberated in her brain. "That's good."

They turned into her bedroom, and Ashley sank down on the bed. His arms left her, and she resisted the urge to reach out to him. Instead, she laid back and closed her eyes. She didn't have enough energy to lift her little finger.

"You going to sleep in your clothes?" he asked, voice still low and sexy in the quiet room.

"Yeah." Sadly, there was no reason to take them off.

"At least take off your shoes." He crouched down on the floor, and his hands went to work on the straps of her sandals. His fingers were strong and sure, and she felt a sigh seep out of her.

After a minute, he slipped them off. Then he tugged at the bottom of her thigh-high stocking.

Though his touch stayed well below her knee, the stocking band slid slowly, erotically down her thigh, caressing her skin. She had to fight a gasp.

Then he let the stocking float to the floor, and took her bare foot in his hand. He rubbed the pad of his thumb firmly up her arch—once, then twice. Starting at her heel, and working his way toward her toes, massaging away the stiffness and the tension that had built up over the day.

Her skin warmed and tingled under the friction of his touch, and she moaned in appreciation.

"Good?" he asked huskily.

"Oh, yeah." Fight or not, there was no denying this was *good*.

A few minutes later, he switched to the other foot.

Again, he slowly drew off her stocking. Then he rubbed and flexed and stroked her skin until her body dissolved to jelly.

After long minutes, he released her foot and stood up.

She opened her eyes to find him standing over her, staring at her, unblinking and silent.

"I have to go," he finally said. There was regret in his expression. Regret, and an echo of her own desperate longing deep in his eyes.

Her heartbeat deepened.

This was it.

He was leaving her apartment now.

Then tomorrow, he was leaving California.

They'd go to the office, and he'd either try to get Jeffrey the job, or he'd give it up to Carl. But, one way or the other, Jordan would be on a plane to Alaska, and she'd be left here all alone.

The realization filled her with a sudden fear.

"Don't go," she whispered.

His eyes widened in surprise.

She reached for his hand, wrapping her fingers around his, holding tight. "Stay."

His voice trembled slightly. "You sure?"

She nodded.

He crouched down beside her, taking her hand between his and lifting it to his lips for a gentle kiss. "I'd like nothing better than to crawl into bed with you right now. But you need to sleep."

"I will sleep." She stared into his eyes. They might disagree on what to do tomorrow, but she didn't care. The next few hours were all they had left, and she wasn't willing to give them up. "Whatever happens tomorrow, hold me in your arms tonight."

His lips curved into a slow smile, and his irises seemed to light from within. "Nothing I'd rather do."

He slipped out of his shoes, tossed his tie on the chair, and lay down on his back beside her, drawing her close with a strong arm and guiding her head to his chest.

"You feel *so* good," he breathed. "I missed you so much."

Ashley's chest contracted. That was it. She missed him. Only a few hours apart, and she'd missed him desperately.

She let out a slow breath, slipped her arm across his chest, and let her body melt against his. "You feel good, too."

His steady heartbeat echoed in her ears.

She closed her eyes and pretended he wasn't going away. She pretended they could stay like this forever—and that her world and his world weren't going to intrude.

"I hate that we're fighting," he whispered in her ear.

She put her fingers to his lips. "We're not fighting right now."

He captured her hand, kissing the tip of her index

finger, then her middle finger, then her ring finger, then her baby finger. "I'm glad."

Argonaut Studios no longer existed. "Tell me some more about Alaska."

"Sure." He gathered her hand against the warmth of his neck and held it there.

"What do you want to know?"

"Is it beautiful?"

"Oh, yeah." His voice took on a musical lilt. "Especially in the summer. When the days get long. The ice melts, the leaves nearly burst onto the trees. We have twenty hours of daylight in May. You can practically watch the garden grow."

"*Twenty* hours?"

"At the solstice, in June, in never really gets dark. You can garden or play golf at midnight."

"Which do you do?"

"Neither. I usually sleep."

"In broad daylight?"

"You get used to it. Though it's easy to forget about the time. Once, I was down by the lake, chopping firewood. It must have been about one in the morning, and all of a sudden, the dogs started barking up a storm."

"You have dogs?"

"Yeah."

"I always wanted a puppy."

"You've never had a dog?"

Ashley shook her head. "My dad said they were too

much trouble. Of course we lived in an apartment, but I would have settled for a toy poodle or a Shih Tzu."

"Up in Alaska, we have a name for those little, poofty dogs."

"What is it?"

"Flushables."

She nudged him with her elbow. "That's terrible. Poor little things."

Jordan just chuckled.

"What kind of dogs do you have?" she asked.

"Husky-German shepherd cross, near as I can tell."

"Where are they now?"

"At the cabin."

"By *themselves?*"

"Tushi and Taku are smart enough to head down to the neighbor's for dinner if I don't show up."

"Won't they freeze?"

"They have a doghouse."

She pulled back and gave him an accusing look. "You are cruel and inhuman."

"I am not."

"It's twenty below up there."

"It's lined with straw."

"Those poor dogs."

"You worry too much. The dogs are fine. They've lived their whole life outside. You want to hear the end of my story or what?"

"Okay."

"Good." He settled her against him once again.

"So I'm chopping away, and the dogs start barking like crazy. I assumed they'd spotted a squirrel. Taku goes rushing past me with Tushi hot on his heels.

"Next thing I know, something's scrabbling up a tree behind me. Honestly, it sounded like the biggest squirrel in the world. I turned around, and saw that they'd treed a bear. Not thirty feet away."

"You have *bears* in your yard?"

"Not often. They're usually just passing through. But I was pretty impressed with the dogs."

"I'll say."

"Still want a poodle?"

"Yes," she said defiantly. "There are no bears in my apartment."

Jordan glanced around her bedroom. "My dogs would tear this place to pieces in an afternoon."

"Your dogs are uncivilized."

He chuckled. "Kind of like their owner."

She gave him another playful nudge. "You know that's not true. Tell me some more."

"What else do you want to hear?"

"What's Alpine like?"

"Small. Spectacular scenery. The people are friendly and funny. We have everything from mountain men to Web site developers living there. I like to think of it as the best of both worlds."

Ashley sighed. "I guess you can't wait to get home."

"Hey." He tipped her chin up. "I like California, too."

For some reason, his words made her feel better. "What do you like about it?"

He gazed off into space. "It's exciting. It's also beautiful. The weather can't be beat. The people are a little complicated. Some of them are downright scary." He paused, refocusing on her. "But others are smart and sexy and fun and gorgeous."

He lifted her hand again, turning it toward him, placing a long, tender kiss on her sensitive palm. "Some are more gorgeous than others."

Her heart fluttered and her toes started to curl. This was exactly how it should be. Her and Jordan, cuddled together, laughing together like lovers.

Like two people in love.

Is this what it would feel like?

Then he shifted her hand to kiss the inside of her wrist, his lips hot on her pulse point.

She took a deep breath and her eyes closed. Too bad they were only pretending.

"You should sleep," he said.

She quickly opened her eyes again, nowhere near ready to relinquish the fantasy. "I'm not tired."

He brushed her hair from her face. "You are such a bad liar."

Falling asleep in Jordan's arms had a deliciously seductive appeal, but she couldn't let it happen just yet. Because as soon as she drifted off, it would be morning and her fantasy would end.

He'd leave, and she'd never again feel his strong

arms around her. She'd never inhale his musky scent, hear his deep voice rumbling in her ear or taste his sweet kisses.

"I want to talk for a while longer," she said.

"Okay, then you tell me about California."

"You're *in* California."

"I mean your California. What do you love? What do you hate?"

Ashley thought about that. "I love the weather. I love the beach. There are a million things to do. Great restaurants, good clubs, top-notch entertainment."

She closed her eyes again, focusing on the warmth of his body and the sound of his heartbeat. "In the summer, it gets very dark at night. And the cool air flows in off the Pacific. The heat of the day disappears, and you can sip fine wine and watch the sunset over the waves from a restaurant deck. You'll swear you've died and gone to Heaven."

His arm tightened around her and his voice dropped. "That's how I'm going to picture you. When I'm sitting alone in my cabin, watching a blizzard rage outside the window, I'll picture you on a deck overlooking the ocean, a glass of wine in your hand, thinking you're in Heaven."

Ashley felt a shiver of dread.

Jordan in Alaska, her in California.

Suddenly the restaurant image didn't seem very much like Heaven.

She tilted her head and stared into his eyes.

He was leaving. He was leaving tomorrow, and there wasn't a thing she could do about it.

She lifted her hand and rubbed it tightly against his cheek, trying to memorize the feel of his skin. Her breath caught in her throat and she stretched up to meet him. "Kiss me," she said. "Make me feel Heaven."

"Sure thing." The words had barely left his lips before he swooped in for a kiss. It was wide and hard and deep.

His fingers made their way into her hair, holding her tight while his tongue plundered. While they kissed, he shifted on the bed. They were face-to-face, chest to chest, thigh to thigh.

Arousal spiraled between them.

"I need to feel your skin," he rasped, plucking one button, then another and another.

Yes. Definitely. Skin was essential.

He stripped off her blouse and then her skirt. When she was lying in her pink bra and low-cut, matching panties, he took a deep breath, slowly skimming the flat of his hand across her stomach, over her navel, down toward the satin and lace.

"You're incredible," he breathed, dipping his fingers beneath the edge.

His fingers found her, teased her, stroked her. Arousal rushed through her bloodstream.

She wanted to squeeze him hard, hold him tight,

make long and amazing love with him so the memory would linger in her bedroom forever.

She started on his buttons. "I want your skin."

"No problem." He quickly pushed off his clothes, then peeled away the last of hers.

Starting at the top, he kissed every inch of her body—her thighs, her belly, her breasts, leaving damp circles to cool her heated skin. When she was squirming and breathless, barely able to utter his name, he braced himself on his elbows, staring down at her with passion-filled eyes. His body was a delicious weight pressing her into the mattress.

"So *good*," he whispered.

She wanted to agree, but the words wouldn't form.

Instead, she pulled up to burrow her face in his neck, needing to breathe his musky scent, to taste his salty skin. He kissed the curve of her collarbone, the swell of her breast. Tucking his forearm beneath her, his lips closed over the tip of her nipple, and a shot of desire rocked her body. Her knees tightened around him.

He moved then. Easing into her, slowly filling her. Every nerve ending reached out to meet him.

Impatient, her fingertips dug into his back, urging him into a faster rhythm.

Her vision tunneled. Small pulses throbbed along her inner thighs. Her skin turned hot, then cold, then hot again, and she arched and reached, curling her toes.

He stroked her hair, kissed her face, his breathing growing deep and labored as he whispered endearments, over and over, and over again.

Finally, he cried out her name, setting off fireworks in the back of her mind, filling her body with hot, endless pleasure.

As she floated down from the pinnacle, she clung to his slick body.

"Don't go," she whispered hoarsely.

"I'm not going anywhere, sweetheart."

"Tomorrow. I know they need you in Alaska, but don't go tomorrow. Stay a little bit longer."

She heard his long sigh. And he held her tight for a full minute, so tight that neither of them could breathe. Then he loosened his arms and pulled back a few inches, touching his forehead to hers.

"I wish I could."

"Are you sure you can't?" Her voice dropped to a whisper. "This... Us... It's something."

He nodded. "I know. That's what scares me. If I stay, it'll get stronger."

Ashley bit her lip. It could. It might.

His dark eyes burned into hers, and he shook his head sadly. "It'll get stronger. And then what will we do?"

10

MORNING CAME far too early.

From where he lay, with Ashley curled against him, Jordan could see her radio alarm. The minutes were rapidly counting down. It was almost six o'clock, and he had to go to Jeffrey's and change before work.

There were only four hours until the meeting with the Board.

He'd racked his brain half the night, but he couldn't think of any sure way to secure Jeffrey's and Ashley's futures. She was right when she said the Board members weren't going to believe him without proof. And going up against Carl, hoping to win the promotion, was simply too big a risk to take.

He buried his face in Ashley's hair, inhaling deeply. He thought about making love with her one last time, but he didn't dare. He was already thinking crazy things, impossible things about Ashley and a future. She was the most intelligent, most daring, most beautiful woman he'd ever met, and he didn't know how he was going to let her go.

He forced himself to rein in the torturous thoughts.

They'd only known each other four days. It was impossible to fall in love that fast.

This had to be infatuation. And, he'd get over an infatuation.

His life was in Alaska, and hers was in California. He had a business and employees, she had a career. No amount of wishing would change those fundamental facts.

He was leaving today, and that was that.

He skimmed his fingertips over her stomach, trying to memorize the softness of her skin, concentrating on the feel of her warm body. She smelled like delicate flowers, and she looked so small cuddled up against him.

Love or not, he was suddenly overwhelmed with the need to protect Ashley from Carl's plotting and scheming. He couldn't forget the ugly expression on the man's face when he'd called her a nonstarter.

There *had* to be a way to resolve this before he left for Alaska.

But, what could he do?

What should he do?

If this was Alaska, *what* would he do?

Hell, that was easy. If something like this happened on his home turf, he'd slam Carl up against the nearest wall and force him to confess for all to hear.

Jordan paused.

His eyebrows twitched.

Could it be that simple?

It wouldn't be pretty, and it would definitely lack finesse. But...

Ashley's radio alarm clicked in.

Maybe...

She stirred in his arms.

It wasn't like he had a whole lot of other options.

She smiled and stretched. "Hi, you."

He smiled in return and placed a slow kiss on her temple. "Hey, yourself. You're looking beautiful."

"You lie."

"I'm serious."

"Right," she drawled."

"I have to go to Jeffery's and change."

The smile went out of her eyes. "So soon?"

He nodded, brushing his hand along her cheek. God, she was beautiful. He'd give anything to be able to stay.

"I want you to know," he whispered close to her ear. "I heard what you said about knowing this business better than me. I respect your opinion, and I'm not going to rush to the Board with unproven allegations."

She opened her mouth to speak.

"But," he quickly continued. "I also can't take the chance of going up against Carl. There's too much to lose."

When she tried to speak again, he put his finger to her lips. "See, we're both right, which means neither of our solutions will work."

"But—"

"I have an idea."

"You do?"

He nodded. "It's not without risk." And Jordan wasn't even completely sure it was legal.

"What are you going to do?" she asked.

"It's better if you don't know."

WITH THE HOURS quickly ticking down, Jordan opened the door to Carl's office at Metro Productions and walked right in.

Carl stood up from his desk. "What are you doing here?"

Jordan locked the door. "I came to find out if you're bluffing."

Carl drew back. "What are you talking about?"

Jordan took a couple of steps toward him, letting the back of his hand brush the tiny tape recorder hidden in his jacket pocket. The hard lump reassured him.

"Talk is cheap," he said. "You're asking me to take a huge leap of faith here. I'm going to need more specifics than 'the right people' and 'everything is in place.'"

Carl folded his arms across his chest. "You don't think I can pull it off?"

"How am I supposed to know if you can or not? Who are the people? What's in place?"

"You don't need to know that yet."

Jordan disagreed. He needed to know that right now. And he needed for Carl to spell it out in no uncertain terms.

"Humor me," said Jordan.

Carl stared hard, remaining stoically silent.

Jordan moved closer still. He wanted to make sure the tape recorder picked up anything and everything that might help him. "You're asking me to give up a really big opportunity here."

"For a really big payoff," said Carl.

"Who's on board?" asked Jordan.

Carl hesitated.

"Are we partners or not?" asked Jordan.

"You're going to have to trust me."

Damn.

Carl remained mulishly silent.

This wasn't working, and Jordan had only one play left.

He shrugged his shoulders and turned to leave, going for broke. "Hope you've got a great pilot to present today, because I'm going to—"

"Wait."

Thank God.

He turned back.

"We've got David Adams," said Carl.

Jordan pretended to be impressed by the name. "How much are we guaranteed?"

Carl sighed hard. "Your cut? Five thousand for the effort, fifteen if the show gets picked up."

That sounded pretty concrete and specific to Jordan. He only hoped it would be enough to convince Harold Gauthier.

THE BOARD OF DIRECTORS at Argonaut listened attentively while Jordan began Jeffrey's pilot series presentation of *Sixty Below*.

He carefully explained how the concept combined the drama and splendor of the Alaskan wilderness with the quirky, colloquial attitudes and behaviors of small-town Alaskans. He clicked the mouse on his laptop computer and a rustic, picturesque small town appeared on the big screen at the far end of the room.

He told them how *Sixty Below* referred to both the icy cold temperatures found in Alaska and to the sixtieth parallel, above which most of Alaska sat. He talked about the town of Arctic Luck, and clicked through some still photos of the town.

He introduced Rick Johansen, a New York stockbroker who'd cashed out of his Manhattan brokerage, left his Madison Avenue wife to head for the wilds of Alaska.

On the surface, it was a fish-out-of-water story, with plenty of quirky northern characters interacting with Rick as he tried to acclimatize. But the drama came from his former wife's desire to win him back, and her father's mob connections. Nina was Rick's ex-wife, and a mob bodyguard had been sent by her father to look after her.

The bodyguard had a crush on Nina, and he was extremely jealous of Rick.

Jordan then went through a series of clips from the first six episodes.

The clips were fairly self-explanatory, so Jordan simply watched along with the rest. Rob and Ashley had done a very impressive job. The presentation was smooth, coherent and interesting. If Jordan was a television executive, he'd definitely be interested.

When the last clip finished, he shut off the equipment and turned up the lights.

"Very nice," said the gray-haired Harold Gauthier with a nod.

The rest of the men around the table either agreed or were following Harold's lead, because heads began nodding.

"Thank you," said Jordan, feeling very guilty about taking credit.

"Any other questions for Jeffrey?" Harold asked the other Board members.

"How was New York?" asked one of them.

"Cold," said Jordan. "I'm glad to get back before another winter sets in."

The men laughed and, luckily, didn't pursue the topic.

"I guess we can take a short break before we talk to Carl," said Harold, pushing back from his chair.

Jordan braced himself. "This might be presumptuous,'' he said to Harold. ''But could I speak with you for a moment?''

Harold looked surprised, and he stared at Jordan for a moment. ''Sure,'' he said. He glanced around at the others. ''Can you gentlemen excuse us for a moment.''

The room cleared, and the door shut behind the last man.

Harold sat back. ''What can I do for you?''

Jordan took a deep breath. ''May I speak frankly?''

''Of course.''

''Good. I'd like to make it clear that I don't expect you to take any of what I'm about to tell you at face value. I would fully hope that you'd investigate the matter independently, and come to your own conclusions.''

Harold shifted back in his chair. ''This sounds ominous.''

''It is,'' Jordan agreed. ''It's come to my attention that Carl Nedesco is planning to commit a crime.''

Harold's eyebrows shot up.

''I know I have some very strong reasons for wanting to discredit him right now. But, I swear to you, I'm not making this up.''

''A crime would be a pretty outrageous thing to make up,'' said Harold.

''He offered me a bribe,'' said Jordan. ''He bribed me to throw this job competition in return for the title of senior acquisitions director and twenty-five percent of the take."

Harold leaned forward. "The take of what?"

"I think he's going to accept bribes from studios. He alluded to the Verona scam, and he told me he had the right people in the right places. I let him think I'd go along with it."

"Why didn't you come to me sooner?"

"I had no proof before this morning. And I had no opportunity to see you alone before now."

"You have proof?"

Jordan set the tape recorder on the table in front of Harold. "I think so."

He hit the play button.

He and Carl's conversation played back into the cavernous boardroom.

"The voice definitely sounds like Carl," said Harold.

Jordan hit the stop button. "He's probably hidden everything very well. And I honestly don't know how you'd independently verify it without giving him the job. And I do have a vested interest in discrediting him. But for the sake of your shareholders and your employees, you deserve to know this before you make a decision."

Harold nodded decisively. "I know you wouldn't manufacture evidence, Jeffrey."

Jordan nodded. His brother had obviously earned

credibility with some very important people. "Thank you for that."

Harold stood up and stuck out his hand. "I don't think I'm going out on too much of a limb if I welcome you to the vice president's position."

Jordan stared at Harold's hand. So fast? Just like that?

"Before you make that offer," said Jordan, coming to a quick decision, the first truly right decision he'd come to in days. "I think there's something else you should see."

Harold dropped his hand. "More criminals lurking in the wings?"

Jordan shook his head. "Ashley Baines's presentation."

"Ashley indicated to me that she doesn't want the job," said Harold. "And, quite honestly, I don't think she's ready. With a little more experience, she has a bright future ahead of her, but—"

"Vice president's candidate or not, you should take a look at her pilot series."

"She can add it to the list for next month's meeting. I'd have no problem with that."

"I think you should take a look at it today."

Harold's eyes narrowed, and Jordan wondered if he'd gone too far.

"I'd really appreciate it," said Jordan.

After a moment's consideration, Harold nodded.

"Okay. If it's that important to you. Since we have a little flex in the meeting schedule."

He pushed a button on the intercom, and asked the secretary to send the other Board members back in.

This morning, when Jordan had realized that he and Ashley's presentations were on the same disk, he'd watched enough of it to know that it was good.

And now, he was glad he had.

After Harold explained the situation about Carl, Jordan clicked through the still pictures of Ashley's presentation, then he moved on to the clips.

The men around the boardroom table chuckled their way through the uptight New York detective stumbling around California. They nodded at each other and smiled at the beach scenes, and they hung on the banter between the two lead characters until the end of the final clip.

"Outstanding," said one of them, as Jordan put the lights up.

"I don't know why she backed out," said another.

Harold looked at Jordan. "She would have given you a run for your money," he said.

Jordan sat back down.

Oh, boy.

He guessed that told him what he had to do next.

Jeffrey was going to be some upset. But, with Carl neutralized, there was no way Jordan could live with himself if he didn't speak up on Ashley's behalf.

The Board members were muttering amongst themselves.

"There's something else I have to tell you," said Jordan.

The room turned silent.

"The analysis of the pilot series I presented earlier. The Q-23s?"

They all watched him with interest.

"That was Ashley's work."

Ten foreheads wrinkled in confusion.

"What are you saying?" asked Harold.

Jordan's stomach clenched with regret for his brother. Right or wrong, he'd just failed Jeffrey. "I'm saying that Ashley did the analyses."

"Why?" asked Harold.

"I've been away. I'm rusty. I was pretty swamped after I got back, and I didn't have time...." The excuses sounded lame, even to Jordan.

"I mean, why are you telling us this?"

Jordan paused, not completely understanding the question. "Because it's not fair to Ashley for me to use her work."

Harold folded his hands on the table and leaned forward. "You do realize the position you've put us in."

"Yes."

"Do you *want* Ashley to get the promotion?

Yes. No. There was no good answer here.

"No," said Jordan. "To be perfectly honest, I wish

I'd been successful. But I can't ethically use her work to further my own career."

"Admirable," said one Board member.

"Insane," said another.

"I've never..." said a third.

Harold picked up the Q-23s that Jordan had submitted. "It seems we may have underestimated Ashley Baines."

There were a series of nods around the table.

Harold smiled and shook his head. "I think we'd better ask Ashley to join the meeting."

11

ASHLEY APPROACHED the boardroom door with trepidation. She couldn't think of a single reason they'd want her to join the meeting.

Unless they'd found out the truth about Jordan.

She tried to quell the butterflies in her stomach.

Maybe he'd told them she helped. Maybe they were going to fire her. They'd probably fire Jeffrey, too. Then Carl would take over the whole department, and her employees and co-workers would suffer.

The butterflies pulled into a tight circle, and her stomach cramped as she reached for the door handle, pulling on the heavy, wooden door.

"Ashley." Harold Gauthier stood up from his seat at the end of the table. "So glad you could join us."

Ashley glanced at the other members of the Board. They were beaming at her.

She sought Jordan, staring into his eyes, silently begging him for information.

He grinned at her as he walked around the table.

He sure didn't look like a man who'd just been fired.

When he got to her, he paused for a split second, letting his knuckles brush against hers.

"Knock 'em dead, tiger," he whispered under his breath.

"Wha—"

Then he opened the door and disappeared.

"Loved *Kissed In California*," said Harold, gesturing for Ashley to sit down in one of the chairs.

Now Ashley was really confused. "How did you..."

"Jeffrey showed it to us."

"He *what*?" Why would Jordan do that? What was he *thinking*?

Harold patted the back of the chair. "Join us, Ashley."

She numbly walked over to the vacant chair and sat down.

Harold took his own seat to her left.

"He also told us you did the pilot analysis."

"I..." Ashley wondered if she was walking into a trap. Why had Jordan been smiling? What was going on here?

"We were very impressed," said Harold. He sat back and cocked his head, considering her. "It appears we've underestimated you."

Ashley glanced around the room, trying desperately to get her bearings. "You have?"

He nodded. "We'd like to offer you the vice president's position."

"But—"

He raised his hand. "Now, I know you told me you wanted to back out. But I think you should seriously consider our offer."

Ashley blinked. "What about Jord...Jeffrey?"

"Jeffrey's fine with it."

Ashley wasn't about to argue with her boss, but she was pretty sure Jeffrey was going to be anything but fine.

"He told us you did the work." Harold shook his head and gave a chuckle of disbelief. "That man has some sense of honor. We were all set to offer him the job, and he forced us to rethink the decision in your favor."

The room started to spin.

Ashley gripped the table for support.

"He sabotaged himself? For *me?*"

"What do you say?"

Jordan had handed her the job. He'd sacrificed Jeffrey's chances for her.

Why?

Why would he do that?

"Ashley?" Harold prompted.

She met his gaze. She hated to do it, but she had to ask. "Carl?"

"Jeffrey had some very interesting information to share with us about Carl."

"Oh?"

"Shall we put in the order for the gold nameplate?" asked Harold, a twinkle in his eyes.

Ashley felt a smile tug at her lips.

This was incredible.

She nodded, unable to get her mind around what had just happened.

Against all odds, she was the new vice president.

Harold stood up and reached out to shake her hand.

Ashley rose, extending her own hand. "Thank you. I'm... This is going to sound crazy, but I have to talk to Jeffrey."

"Go ahead. Can you make a two-thirty meeting in my office?"

"Yes. Sure. Of course."

"See you then."

"JORDAN!" ASHLEY BURST into his office, fearful that he might have left for the airport before she got out of the boardroom. She *had* to see him.

He was walking toward the door, and she rushed to meet him.

"What? Why? How?" She stopped in front of him.

Jordan smiled and shook his head. "In the end, I couldn't do it. I couldn't take credit for all your hard work."

"But, Jeffrey..."

"Will be disappointed, maybe angry. Though I'd like to think he'd have made the same call. Fact is, you *earned* this promotion. You deserve it, and I wasn't about to help him coast in on your effort."

Ashley felt a warm glow come to life inside her. She

braced her hands on his shoulders and stretched up to kiss him. "Thank you," she whispered. Then her voice grew thick in her throat. "No one has *ever* done that for me."

He held her tight. "Done what?"

"Listened to me."

"I'm sure plenty of people have listened to you."

"No. Really listened. I told you what I wanted, and you didn't tell me to stop wanting it. You believed in me. You supported me. You *helped* me."

His voice was thick with emotion. "I want you to be happy, Ashley."

"I am." But her voice cracked over the words. "Oh, Jordan."

"I know." He rubbed his hands up and down her back. "It got stronger anyway, didn't it?"

She nodded against his shoulder, fighting back tears. How was she supposed to say goodbye to him?

He sighed. "I can't see you flying to Alaska on weekends, and my planes won't make it this far...."

He was right. It was the sweetest experience of her life, but it had to end. "I'll miss you," she whispered.

"Every second," he replied.

"This is going to get really sappy if we're not careful," she laughed.

"You're telling me."

She backed off a couple of inches, wiping a wayward tear. "Why don't you tell me what happened with Carl?"

Jordan grinned. "I taped his confession."

"How did you ever get him to confess?"

Jordan cleared his throat. "It wasn't subtle, and I doubt it was legal, but I was fighting for my brother and the woman... I tricked him."

"You're amazing."

"You're biased."

"That's because I—"

He put his fingers over her lips and shook his head. "Goodbye, Ashley. You're going to be a *great* vice president."

Then he turned and quickly walked out the door.

Ashley's confession burned in her throat. She swallowed. Maybe if it remained unsaid, it wouldn't be true.

AT SEVEN O'CLOCK that night, Ashley twisted her key in her apartment door, her body still buzzing from emotional overload.

She didn't know what to do.

She didn't know how to feel.

She'd just been handed her lifetime dream on a silver platter, but somehow the victory didn't feel glorious.

It felt hollow.

Harold had shown her around her new top-floor, corner office, but all she'd been able to do was think of Jordan.

She'd pictured him in a taxi, then on a jet, then driving through the snow and, finally, sitting in his cabin with his dogs, watching the snow fall outside his window.

Was that what he was doing right now?

She stared at her phone.

He had to have one.

If he did, she could call him.

Just to talk.

Just to tell him how the rest of the afternoon had gone.

Just to hear the sound of his voice.

She tossed her purse on the love seat, kicked off her shoes, and picked up the receiver, asking directory assistance for help. She didn't know his address, but there couldn't be more than one Jordan Adamson in Alpine, Alaska.

The operator informed her that there wasn't even one.

No listing for Jordan or J or anything else under Adamson in Alpine, Alaska.

Dejected, she put down the phone.

She could try to find an e-mail address for him, she supposed. Maybe he had one at his airline. But, somehow writing him a note didn't appeal to her.

Instead, she wandered into her bedroom, peeling off her work clothes, climbing into a comfortable old sweatshirt and a pair of tights.

She lay down on the bed, and blinked back a tear.

When the next tear leaked out, she swiped the back of her hand across her face in frustration.

She needed to be celebrating, not wallowing in self-pity.

She rolled over onto her side, and her cheek hit something hard.

Lifting her hand, she felt her way around the pillow, flipping back the quilt to find the offending object.

It was a case.

Ashley sat up, folding her legs beneath her.

It was a flat, rectangular, velvet case.

And there was a note taped to the lid.

With a trembling hand, she peeled the note away and opened the folded paper.

I didn't take everything back to Alaska, was all it said.

Ashley read the words twice, trying to figure out what they could possibly mean.

Stumped, she lifted the velvet lid.

There, nestled on a soft bed of deep purple, was a heart-shaped, diamond necklace.

A heart.

His heart.

Ashley's stomach bottomed out, and her chest squeezed so tight she could barely breathe.

She sprang off the bed.

She had to get to Jordan. And she had to do it *now*.

JORDAN KICKED the snow off his boots as he entered the True North office on Saturday morning.

"Well, it's about time you showed up," said Wally from behind the counter.

"Plane was late," said Jordan. "Didn't get home until three this morning."

"Talk about letting a guy suffer," said a very familiar voice.

Jordan quickly turned to meet Jeffrey's gaze. Cyd was here, too.

His brother took a couple of steps toward him. "It's not like much was at stake or anything."

"Sorry," said Jordan, more sorry than Jeffrey realized.

"So, how'd we do?" asked Jeffrey.

"Well..."

"Never mind." Jeffrey took another step. "Shake your brother's hand before we get to all that."

"You *know?*" asked Jordan, thrown off guard.

Jeffrey firmly grasped Jordan's hand and gave him a couple of slaps on the back. "I celebrated your birthday at the Mush Lodge. We've got an awful lot to talk about, you and me."

Despite the bad news he was about to announce, Jordan couldn't help but smile. His brother. He had a brother.

"Can you stay a few days?" he asked Jeffrey. He wanted to know everything. From Jeffrey's first memory to the moment he set foot in the Alpine airport. They had an entire lifetime to catch up on.

Jeffrey grinned. "Yeah. I can stay. I've grown rather fond of Alaska in the past few days."

"Liked Katimuk did you?"

"*Interesting* friends you've got up there."

The inflection Jeffrey put on the word "interesting" made Cyd sock him in the arm. "Watch it, sweetheart."

Jordan stared at her in bemusement. Sweetheart? Admittedly, it wasn't said in the most affectionate tone. But, *sweetheart?*

Jeffrey laughed, wrapping an arm around Cyd and pulling her in for a kiss. "This is one of the things I liked best about Alaska."

Jordan blinked. "Did I miss something?"

"Did you ever," muttered Wally.

Jordan peered at his tomboy pilot, who'd taken a sudden interest in the departure board and wasn't meeting his eyes.

"Cyd and I have an understanding," said Jeffrey, kissing the top of Cyd's head. "She understands that I love her, and I understand she'll never leave me."

Cyd gave Jordan a fleeting, sheepish glance, then quickly returned her attention to Jeffrey.

The sight of their mutual rapture was like a fist in Jordan's stomach. It had nearly killed him to leave Ashley. He'd thought about her the whole way home.

Did she get the necklace?

Would she call?

Would she think of him?

Would she find another man?

That last thought had filled him with a kind of primitive rage, and it was all he could do to keep from pulling a U-turn in the middle of the highway and heading back to the airport.

Even now, it felt as though there were an invisible tether pulling him back to California. He could only hope the raw need would fade over time.

"Now, about my promotion," said Jeffrey.

Jordan opened his mouth to get the bad news over with, but the reception door burst open with a swirl of ice-fog and a clatter of feet.

The ice-fog cleared, and his fondest wish appeared before his eyes.

"Ashley?" Jordan couldn't believe he was seeing straight.

"Ashley?" Jeffrey echoed.

Her face was bright pink, her hands were stuffed under her arms, and she was shivering with cold.

Jordan quickly stepped forward and pulled her into his arms, rubbing his hands up and down her back. "What are you *doing* here?"

"Freezing," she chattered.

That was an understatement. Her cheeks were frosty against his neck, and her hands were like icicles.

But she was here. He didn't know how, and he didn't much care. She was here, and his arms no longer ached with emptiness.

"Excuse us," he said to Cyd and Jeffrey, brushing

past them, pulling Ashley with him into his office and closing the door behind them.

He grabbed his parka from the hook and wrapped it around her shoulders, feeling hope soar inside him. "Tell me what you're doing here," he said almost desperately.

She snuggled into the depths of the oversize coat, looking up at him with shining, blue eyes. "You promised to take me flying."

Flying?

"Is today okay?"

It took him a minute to sort through her answer.

She was here to go flying?

He smiled, and a wave of happiness rose inside him. She was in Alaska on a ridiculously flimsy excuse, which meant it was for no other reason than to see him.

He didn't know how he'd got so lucky.

"Today's perfect for flying," he said, drawing her, parka and all, into the cradle of his arms.

"What about tomorrow?" she asked, her voice muffled.

"Tomorrow's good, too." He began to rock back and forth. It felt so good to hold her again.

There was a knock at the door. It opened, and Jeffrey's head poked around. "Who got the job?"

"Ashley did," said Jordan.

"But you can have it if you want it," said Ashley.

Jordan drew back. "What?"

She shrugged. "I can't be vice president of Argonaut and still stay here with you."

"You can't give it up," Jordan protested. It was her life, her dream. He'd never ask that of her.

"I'll check back later," said Jeffrey, and ducked back out, closing the door again.

Jordan cupped Ashley's face. "You can't do this."

She pulled her hand out of the parka and lifted his diamond necklace from her throat. "You have my heart, too. I love you, Jordan. And I want to be with you, no matter what."

"Not at the expense of your career."

She tipped her head, considering him. "That wasn't exactly what I expected you to say back."

"Oh. Right. Sorry. I love you, too, Ashley." He bent down to kiss her, squeezing her tight, putting every ounce of his love and passion into the embrace.

She loved him. Ashley Baines loved *him*.

The world didn't get any better than this.

She pulled back and grinned at him. "That's better. Now, about that promise to take me flying...."

"Is that your house down there?" Ashley peered through the frosty glass of the Cessna window at a green-roofed, log cabin with a white plume of smoke chugging out the chimney. It was set in a large clearing by the lakeshore, with a wide porch out front and a few outbuildings behind.

"That's it. Look, you can see Tushi and Taku running down the lake."

Ashley squinted against the bright, white snow, just making out two brown spots.

While Jordan banked to bring the ski plane parallel to his cabin, Ashley scanned the distant landscape. She could just make out the small cluster of buildings that was the town of Alpine. Closer up, were the dozen or so houses that made up his neighborhood. And the long, narrow lake beneath them was an unbroken strip of ice, streaming in a white ribbon down the valley.

She tried to picture it in summer, when the trees were green and the lake thawed blue. She was sure it would be breathtaking.

They lost altitude, and the small town disappeared, while the trees and houses grew bigger. Then they touched down on the snow-covered ice and the Cessna slid to a stop directly in front of the cabin.

While Jordan helped Ashley out of the plane, Taku and Tushi bounded toward them, enthusiastically jumping up and down, and barking and sniffing back and forth from Jordan to Ashley.

"I don't think a poodle is such a good idea after all," Ashley laughed, nearly losing her balance as one of the dogs brushed up against her.

Jordan's expression turned serious as he shut the pilot's door. "You really need to think about this, Ashley. Alaska's not like anything you've ever seen before."

"*You're* not like anything I've ever seen before," she countered. "And I have thought about it. I'm really not getting a poodle."

Jordan captured her mittened hand in his leather glove. "You know what I mean."

She paused. "Yes. I do. And I *have* thought about it. I've had nearly six hours on airplanes to think about it. I've thought about what kind of work I can do in Alaska." She smiled. "I'm pretty sure there'll be a show called *Sixty Below* filmed around here soon."

Jordan shook his head, but she rushed on before he had a chance to speak.

"I've also thought about what I can do long-distance, as a consultant. And about working part-time in California and part-time here."

"It wouldn't be the same," said Jordan. "You'd be turning your career upside down."

Ashley shrugged. "So what?"

"Ashley..."

"Do we have to figure it all out this second? Standing out here in the cold?"

"I'm hoping you'll be reasonable once the wind picks up."

She squeezed his hand. "Whatever happened to 'yes, ma'am'? I think I liked that better. Now, be a gentleman and take me inside."

"Yes, ma'am."

She snuggled up beside him as they walked toward the cabin with the dogs bounding out in front.

A shoveled pathway led to the front stairs and a screened-in porch. There, Jordan pushed open the front door.

It was much bigger than she'd expected, lighter, fresher, with a high, wooden ceiling, an open loft and four big skylights. The log walls were polished a rich honey color, reflecting the orange flames which danced behind the glass door of the woodstove. The furniture was supple leather with colorful throw rugs and pillows scattered in every corner.

Through an archway, she could see a completely modern kitchen. And Jordan's computer desk was tucked away under the stairs.

She breathed a deep sigh of contentment.

She could work here. Happily.

Jeffrey had suggested a job share. He'd even offered to approach Harold. Maybe Harold would go for it. If not, they'd come up with another plan. A plan that would keep her and Jordan together.

"It'll work," she whispered.

Jordan shut the door, leaving the dogs outside. "Ashley..."

She stripped off her mittens and unzipped his coat, slipping her hands into the warmth beneath and pressing her cheek to his flannel shirt.

His arms went around her and he kissed the top of

her head. "Are you sure you'll be happy here? What about succeeding...the corporate ladder?"

She didn't care. She honestly and truly did not care one bit about the corporate ladder. "I'm tired of climbing it," she told Jordan honestly. "I'm tired of working late, competing with *everybody*, and fighting off guys like Carl. I've spent the last fifteen years building my life around my career. And, you know what?"

"What?"

"For the very first time, I want to build my career around my life." She turned to look at him. He was rugged and handsome and sexy and smart, and she was so lucky to love him. A ripple of pure joy raced through her. "You want to help me?"

He held her hands, and his eyes lit up. "Oh, yeah. You want to marry me?"

She grinned. "Definitely, yes."

He bent down, and she stretched up, and the long kiss they shared nearly melted the Alaska winter.

Breathless, he raised his head. "You want a tour of your new bedroom now?"

"Definitely, yes."

*   *   *   *   *

Modern Romance™
...seduction and
passion guaranteed

Tender Romance™
...love affairs that
last a lifetime

Medical Romance™
...medical drama
on the pulse

Historical Romance™
...rich, vivid and
passionate

Sensual Romance™
...sassy, sexy and
seductive

Blaze Romance™
...the temperature's
rising

27 new titles every month.

Live the emotion

MILLS & BOON®

MB3

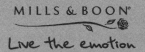

FREE
2 BOOKS
AND A SURPRISE GIFT!

We would like to take this opportunity to thank you for reading this Mills & Boon® book by offering you the chance to take TWO more specially selected titles from the Sensual Romance™ series absolutely FREE! We're also making this offer to introduce you to the benefits of the Reader Service™—

- ★ FREE home delivery
- ★ FREE monthly Newsletter
- ★ FREE gifts and competitions
- ★ Exclusive Reader Service discount
- ★ Books available before they're in the shops

Accepting these FREE books and gift places you under no obligation to buy; you may cancel at any time, even after receiving your free shipment. Simply complete your details below and return the entire page to the address below. *You don't even need a stamp!*

YES! Please send me 2 free Sensual Romance™ books and a surprise gift. I understand that unless you hear from me, I will receive 4 superb new titles every month for just £2.69 each, postage and packing free. I am under no obligation to purchase any books and may cancel my subscription at any time. The free books and gift will be mine to keep in any case.

T4ZEF

Ms/Mrs/Miss/Mr ....Initials ....
BLOCK CAPITALS PLEASE

Surname ....

Address ....

....

....Postcode ....

Send this whole page to:
UK: FREEPOST CN81, Croydon, CR9 3WZ
EIRE: PO Box 4546, Kilcock, County Kildare (stamp required)